MW00769579

MOON TEARS

To Haley,
I hope you enjoy reading this
story and that it inspires you in
your swimming! Happy Reading!

M. M. Frische

M M Frische
9/20/16

Ten Story Books, LLC
Dallas, TX

Copyright © 2014 M. M. Frische
All rights reserved.

Published by Ten Story Books, LLC
P.O. Box 701561, Dallas, TX 75370

Ten Story Books, LLC and the Ten Story Books logo are trademarks
of Ten Story Books, LLC

ISBN-10: 0991634810
ISBN-13: 978-0-9916348-1-1

Library of Congress Control Number: 2014940160

Cover design by Nathan Reinhardt
Cover photo: © Ysign1 | Dreamstime.com

First edition: June, 2014

Summary: Asthma-ridden fourteen-year-old Lou Davis is left behind
to run her remote town when an error in the 1940 census results in
every male over eighteen being drafted and all the women leaving to
work in factories.

No part of this book may be reproduced, scanned, transmitted, or
distributed in any form or by any means, whether electronic or
mechanical, without written permission of the publisher. For
information regarding permission, write to Ten Story Books, LLC,
Attention: Permissions, P.O. Box 701561, Dallas, TX 75370.

Please purchase only authorized editions.
Ten Story Books appreciates your support of the author's rights.
For questions or more information, contact us at
info@tenstorybooks.com.

Thank you for purchasing this Ten Story Books, LLC publication.
www.tenstorybooks.com

To Lou,
for sharing your life stories,
allowing me to write about them,
and inspiring me to grasp life by the horns.

CHAPTER 1

November, 1941

I can't...breathe. I sputtered between gulps of the nearly frozen water and struggled not to drown. Each stroke in the frigid liquid felt thick and exhausting. Every boisterous breeze prickled my skin. Sometimes I wanted the asthma to win so I could sink into the icy darkness forever. Only the kicking kept me from descending to the lake's icy depths where denizens of the deep waited to nibble bits of my frozen flesh for breakfast.

"Keep going, Lou," Papa said from the rowboat beside me, stroking the water rhythmically with his oars. "You're almost there."

"*I can't,*" I coughed out, stopping to tread water and catch my breath. A rude wave shoved my head, and water plunged into my lungs. Coughs wracked my body. I jerked back as the scales of a fish scraped across my thigh. My stomach muscles ached. But Papa wouldn't stop rowing.

Even if I had to break ice every morning on the edge of this God-forsaken lake just to get into the water, I had to swim across it. One endless mile. Three hundred and sixty-five days a year. Doctor's orders.

Blasted asthma, I thought.

I treaded water as long as I could get away with it. Every inch of my fourteen-year-old body chattered.

"The quicker you swim, the quicker you can get in the boat," Papa said.

I rolled my eyes and stuck out what must have been a purple tongue.

"Don't roll those baby blues at me, girl. Now swim."

Easy for him to say. I began performing the familiar strokes like the ingrained ritual they were. Water sluiced over my head and trickled down into my ears. My arms sliced through the crystal clear water as I imagined I was in the ocean. The warm, salty, undulating ocean. For a moment, I actually began to feel warmer. *Just a little bit farther...*

I focused on the fog drifting across the waves that promised the shoreline. The water gently rose and fell taking me with it.

A glance over my shoulder rewarded me with the first rays of morning sunlight. The fog began to dissipate as I turned back toward the shoreline. In front of me, Mount Callisto, the valley's ancient volcano, shimmered and twinkled, betraying the treasures of her slopes.

Time to start the countdown, I thought. *Five, four, three, two, one...*

I gave a final kick and made shore. My wrinkled hands and feet, oversized prunes, dug into the black, silky sand. The cool, dark grains squished between my toes, and I made a beeline for the drier sand, which coated my feet as I trudged up the hill ahead.

"Okay," said Papa, pulling the boat onto shore. "Run get one."

As my daily reward for the forced swim, Papa let me collect one diamond. From the lake, the diamonds looked like jewels of the Gods, dancers among the fire. Up close, the gems appeared murky, rough, uncut. They looked nothing like the shiny, perfectly cut stones found in fancy San Francisco stores. Most people walked right by them, mistaking them for glass. But they looked beautiful to me, felt smooth and strong. I ran my finger along each edge, felt every groove, admired their strength and toughness.

"Good job this morning. Let's head back." Papa ruffled my wet head and wrapped me in an Indian blanket the tribal chief gave him last winter.

After one more glimpse at forty-two hundred feet of shimmering slopes, I snuggled into the bottom of the boat, away from the wind that rises with the sun. Papa pushed away from shore with one oar, singing a new Bing Crosby tune. It was always Bing Crosby.

"Where the turf meets the surf," he crooned.

"Very funny, Papa."

The croon waned to a hum. All part of the daily routine. The trek back across the lake was much quicker than the way over. The scent of the water ignited my senses instead of filling my lungs. The mist lifted off the lake like an airplane taking to the sky. Birds skirted the heavens above us and welcomed the new day. Nature arose, and life filled the valley.

A distant hum began to overtake the morning calls of mockingbirds, and I heard a break in the rhythm of Papa's oars. I glanced up to see his steel gray eyes stare in the direction of the hum. A strange bird skimmed the mountain and descended toward the lake. Toward us.

We watched. Papa's grip on the oars tightened. His bushy brows grew closer, and his eyes shifted into the look he cast at buzzards.

A seaplane rocked and yawed overhead. Tucking the diamond safely into my fist, I shaded my eyes with my other hand to watch the plane. I ducked as the intruder buzzed our boat.

"They're coming in way too steep and banking all wrong," I said. I sat up to study the plane. "They need to put their flaps down. And soon."

I loved planes and would much rather be flying in the morning sky than swimming in morning water. I still remember the first time I saw one of those marvels in the sky. It was a little yellow tandem two-seater and the first plane I ever rode in. I felt like Amelia Earhart. I could close my eyes and feel the wind underneath the wings when that plane lifted off the ground. The local pilots took me for rides when they had extra room and taught me about ailerons, cowlings, carb heat and how to keep those big fabric-and-wood birds up in the sky. The pilot waggling overhead could have definitely used some lessons.

The shadow of the seaplane crossed my face.

"What does that red dot mean?" I asked.

Papa gripped the oars. His stocky arms rowed faster than usual. "It means it's time to get to shore."

CHAPTER 2

"There's Sheriff Gabe." I watched Papa's best friend saunter toward the lake, holding up a badge. His long legs arched outward, looking like he spent more time in the saddle than on the ground. My dog, Silver, trotted close to his heels.

"Looks like you're going to be Deputy Davis today," I said. Papa worked years ago as a federal marshal along the Texas-Mexico border out of El Paso, so he knew what he was doing. Whenever the sheriff needed an extra deputy, he called on him.

"Got a call they was comin' up our way," Sheriff Gabe said. "Thought I could use an extra set of eyes an' ears."

Papa turned to me. "After you tie up the boat, run straight to the house and get ready for school." He nestled the boat against the dock. My fingers worked the corded ropes into sailing knots without thinking as Silver licked my fingertips. The sheriff and Papa both raised their right hands. The swearing in was done before I was.

"Wonder what they're doing here," I said, finishing the last knot. I stepped out of the boat and raced Silver for home.

Behind me, I heard Papa mutter, "Whatever it is, it can't be good."

Silver beat me to the house and curled up in front of the door to my bedroom. I ran through the kitchen and slid into the living room. The stones were cold on my bare feet, so I gingerly danced across them and scurried toward my room. A smoky, caramel scent filled the house. The sizzling and popping of maple bacon on the stove beckoned me to breakfast. My stomach growled in response.

I glanced back toward the kitchen as I tossed the Indian blanket over the deer hide divan. Mama's usual smile was missing. Her brows were furrowed as she poured over what looked to be a really long letter.

"What's that?" I asked, nearly tripping over Silver, my constant companion. I leapt over him at the last second and soared into my room. "Sorry, boy." Silver was half-coyote. His silver-gray fur camouflaged with the stone floor Mama and Papa laid through most of the house. White fur peeked through to cover his ruff, blaze, feet and the tip of his tail that twirled in circles like a propeller. I probably should have named him "Prop."

Silver sauntered over to rest on the blue checked blanket he'd slept on since the Indians gave him to me when I was six. He wouldn't sleep anywhere but in my bedroom. Not in my bed, but on the floor next to it. He was my protector. My defender. But Papa didn't like him because, like me, he wouldn't hunt.

"Nothing to worry about," Mama muttered, flapping the letter in the air before laying it on the top corner of Great-Grandma's mahogany cupboard. A blue and red flannel plaid shirt and clean dungarees waited for me at the foot of the same bed I'd slept in since I was three. Mama hated that I wore dungarees instead of dresses, but she knew they were the only thing I'd wear every day of the week except Sunday.

How many pilots wore dresses? I thought. *Jeepers, Amelia Earhart never wore dresses.*

I was toweling off the remnants of lake water when I heard a plate crash on the floor followed by something I never thought I would hear. Mama swore. She never swore. I changed quickly, padded back to the kitchen, and sat down at the table set for seven instead of the usual three. The checkered table cloth hosted the "most important meal of the day" as Mama reminded me *every single morning.* Except for that morning. Something was wrong.

Five thick slices of my favorite bacon lay on my plate. Salty, thick, and crispy. Next to them, Mama placed perfectly browned toast slathered with fresh butter and a spoonful of last season's pear preserves. A glass of lake water and a soggy egg that had an early morning meeting with the floor rounded out breakfast. I shoveled in the food as we watched the plane taxi to the dock behind our house. Mama wiped her hands down the front of her frayed calico apron, then folded her arms across her body, tapping her fingers to a beat I couldn't hear. Another swear word escaped her pursed lips.

With breakfast safely tucked away and keeping my belly company, Mama gave me a nod. I caught a glimpse of the return address on an envelope just about to fall off the end of the table. *US Census Office, Washington D.C.* Mama helped a lot with the 1940 Census, gathering information from everyone in Claret Lake. Being the perfectionist she was, she checked and double-checked every piece of information. *Why would they be writing her?* But my curiosity about our morning visitors trumped my curiosity about what was in that letter, so I kept the question locked away for another day.

I lifted my gray wool coat off the hall tree. I slipped on last year's snow boots and opened and closed the back door quickly enough for Silver and me to scoot outside. We jogged over to the three-foot tall stone wall Papa built between our house and the lake, climbed up, and studied the plane and its pilot. He obviously needed some more flying lessons.

"Silver, I bet they're spies sent on a secret mission. Let's sneak down, stowaway on their plane and put a kink in their plans. I bet they're flying to Canada. Or Mexico. Or Costa Rica. I've always wanted to go to Costa Rica." My mind conjured up all sorts of expeditions to go on. Silver and me climbing the Alps. Canoeing down the Amazon. Dipping our toes in the Arctic Ocean.

"*Woof. Woof.*" Silver greeted Sheriff Gabe.

The lawman sauntered over, wiped a handful of snow off the wall and settled in beside me. He dusted the snow from his gloves and chuckled. "Nice flour." He got a kick out of his favorite "first snow" story at my expense. Mama, Papa and I were in Abilene on a rare trip to visit Grandma Davis in Texas. One morning I got up in my pink-flowered flannel nightgown, shuffled over the cold wooden floor to the window in my bare feet, looked out and screamed, "Someone threw flour all over the front yard!" My parents and Sheriff Gabe loved telling everyone that story, every single year when it started snowing.

The sheriff's attempt at being lighthearted failed as his hands fidgeted so much he stuck them in his pockets, taking an open envelope and letter with them.

Why was everyone getting letters? I thought. Looking up at his leathery face, I asked, "So, who are they?"

"Japanese emissaries," Sheriff Gabe drawled in his native Texan accent. "On their way to Washington D.C. to talk to President Roosevelt. They're makin' sure we ain't goin' to war. Couldn't land in 'Frisco bay for the fog, so they headed up here. D.C.'s sending a plane for 'em. Should be here by noon."

He talked on his two-way radio and rounded up a group of local farmers with plows to clear the valley's dirt strip airport. After last night's storm, snow blanketed the runway like one of Mama's thick winter quilts. He had parked his black-and-white sheriff's car next to our house, ready to take the visitors to the airstrip after he offered them some of Mama's "most important meal of the day." As Mama said, it's always good to be neighborly.

Two men in overcoats and the pilot in a military-looking uniform climbed down one after the other onto the dock just this side of the pump house. It took a moment for their sea legs to get adjusted before they found their land legs. The wind blew through the valley, gusting at about forty knots, making for some pretty choppy air. The pilot handed Papa a couple of bulging paper sacks. Papa hesitated for a moment, then set them down gently behind the oars on the dock.

Sheriff Gabe leaned over and said, "Looks like they might not be partaking in a meal any time soon." Papa led the group up the dock and onto the snow-covered yard. Snow crunched under our boots as we jumped off the wall and walked out to meet them.

"Gabe, Lou, meet Mr. Yamakuto. He is an emissary from Japan." Papa narrowed his eyes, issuing me a silent order. I extended my hand.

"Nice to meet you, sir," I said.

Mr. Yamakuto was a short man, almost as short as I was. He placed a wooden cane across the sleeve of his coat, then lifted a black derby hat from his head with one hand and shook mine with the other. Behind round spectacles, his eyes drooped downward toward his sparse mustache. His skin appeared to be a dull shade of green, but his smile looked friendly enough. Even so, tension filled the air like fog fills 'Frisco Bay. Although the war in Europe was thousands of miles away from northern California, outsiders still made me nervous. My arms prickled with leftover goose bumps.

"Time for school," Papa said. He hugged me and gave the usual peck on the cheek.

"Do you think we're going to war?" I whispered in his ear.

"No idea," he said quietly, and let me go.

He may not have known, but I had my suspicions.

12

CHAPTER 3

June, 1942

About ten days after the emissaries left, Pearl Harbor was hit. Papa said countries never tell their emissaries anything, so they didn't know about the attack. They assumed their country worked in good faith. It's the ambassadors who know everything. Papa said it's like when we sent former presidents on trips overseas, important people on special assignments to try to handle special issues. Of course, we didn't know when the emissaries came through Claret Lake that the Japanese were planning to attack Pearl Harbor. Their country lied to them and sent them to stall us until they could do their dastardly deed.

Luckily, my life had been virtually untouched by the war. I still swam every morning, went to school, and worked at my parents' restaurant and grocery store in the afternoons. Mama and Papa temporarily closed the dance hall they had built along with the restaurant when they first moved to Claret Lake. Not many people wanted to celebrate. Catching a ride in a plane proved as rare as a full tank of gasoline since the government rationed fuel, but I snuck away and talked any pilot that landed at the airstrip into as many minutes up in the air as I could get.

Before the war, I only washed dishes in the Claret Lake Café and Grocery. It seemed I couldn't escape water and prune hands. Then the war came and brought me a promotion. My afternoons included delivering food to round tables covered with red-checked tablecloths, keeping water glasses filled to the brim, and thanks to a growth spurt, stocking the top grocery shelves in the back room.

"Break time," I said to Silver, stepping down from the ladder. "Soda pop and candy bars, coming right up." We snuck under the counter, swiped a few chocolate bars, caramel squares, and soda pops. Chocolate was my major vice in life, besides flying. Mama and Papa were so busy working that they didn't know I hid out, ate all that candy, and drank soda pop until I belched.

"Grab my coat, would 'ya?" I'd been training Silver to fetch. He took my coat in his mouth, meeting me at the door to the icebox.

"You're lucky to have a warm coat built in." I snuggled into my wool coat, and we snuck into the icebox. A wooden latch resided inside, and I pushed against it until the door was almost shut, but not all the way. I didn't want to get stuck in there.

The Café was the only restaurant in town, so my parents designed it with a large storage room in the back with an icebox, which was more of an ice *room*, lined with planks from sturdy, local valley oak trees. Big blocks of ice lined the walls from floor to ceiling to keep the food fresh.

I snuggled down and leaned on a big slab of slippery ice. Silver warmed my feet, and I pulled the stash of candy from my coat pockets. I tossed a pinch of caramel to Silver first, then dove into the chocolate. I was well into my third bar when I heard footsteps approach the door. I stopped mid-chew and willed them to keep walking. Silver whined.

"Shush," I whispered, stroking his fur and holding a finger to my lips. His ears stood at attention, and he stared at the door, every muscle in his body taut. I was barely able to peek through the tiny crack of the door beside me. I could see just enough to make out a figure passing back and forth in front of the ice room. I closed my eyes and put my ear closer to the crack, straining to hear anything. Mumbling soon broke the silence, then two deep voices joined the conversation. I would know those voices anywhere.

"Oh, good, you're both here," Mama said. "We have a serious problem. Read this." Silence filled the room, broken only by the crinkle of paper against rough hands.

"Does this mean what I think it means?" Papa questioned.

"'Fraid so. Got the same letter myself today," Sheriff Gabe murmured. "Don't know what to tell 'ya, Ben. Every last one of us has to go."

"This is ridiculous," Papa said. "I'm fifty years old for crying out loud. I knew those Japanese emissaries were up to no good. That, Pearl Harbor, and now this. I can't believe we are being sucked so far into this war. What is going to happen to the town?"

Mama spoke next. "All I know is that now every male over eighteen from Lagune County's been drafted. *Every single one.*"

"Every single one?" Papa said. "How can that be?"

"I received a letter from the Census Bureau the day the emissaries showed up," Mama said. "Nearest I can figure, the people in Washington made a huge mistake. It appears our *government* doesn't understand basic math and made an error with their decimal points on the last census. Now, their records show Lagune County has a population of *four-hundred* thousand instead of *forty* thousand. Because of one lousy zero, all of the boys and men over eighteen are being drafted. I've been trying to get the clerical error fixed ever since I got this letter, but nobody in D.C. will listen to me. They're too busy rounding up our boys and sending them overseas to fight."

Mama had volunteered to head up the Draft Board, but her duties mostly consisted of trying to comfort the families with sons young enough to be eligible for the draft. "When will Willie be called up? How much notice will we have? When will he be back?" The questions were always the same. Only the names changed. Now, it appeared her problems had just gotten a lot bigger.

So that's what those letters were about, I thought. *That explains Mama's swearing.* I put my ear back up to the crack by the door and heard the clunk of Papa's work boots pacing the room.

Mama spoke again. "Remember how the government wanted to take the eighteen-year-olds, but the nation reared up and wouldn't let that happen for a couple of months?"

"Yeah," the sheriff said. "Then right after they started drafting the eighteen-year-olds, the 'Old Man's Draft' came through. Every one of us between forty-five and sixty-four had to register."

"Supposedly it was only to determine our skills, not for us to actually go to war," Papa said.

Mama spoke up. "Well, it seems with the percentages of draftees calculated the way it is—based on population—they've lumped you all together, and now

17

behind, except for Becky. And Jimmy will be around until he's called up. If we leave old Aunt Mary here, she can oversee the kids' studies. And Doc Tate, of course. Even the army doesn't want a ninety-five-year-old World War I vet. He can take care of any medical emergencies. He may be as old as Methuselah and just about as grouchy, but he's a good one for curing people if he can keep the bottle out of his mouth long enough. And the chief will look out for them—it's just how Rex is."

"That could work, you know," Papa agreed. "They're old enough. They can keep the basics going here."

Without thinking, I tried to swallow what they were saying. But all I swallowed was the unchewed bite of chocolate bar in my mouth. I sputtered and coughed and heard footsteps approaching the icebox. The mammoth door swung open, and Papa pounded on my back until a peanut flew out. He looked down at me, hands on his hips.

"What's this?" he said, glancing at the candy wrappers strewn across the wooden planks.

"Do you—" I sputtered, the chocolate lodging in my throat. "Do you—*all* have to go?"

"'Fraid so, Lou," Mama said, wiping her hands down her apron and shoving letters into her front pocket.

The enormity of what they told me sunk in. "But what will I do without you here?" I started to cry, unable to stop the tears. I must have looked pretty stupid sitting there bawling with my mouth hanging open, half a candy bar in one hand, and chocolate dripping down my chin.

Then it hit, as it always did, out of the blue. Asthma. The monster in my chest.

The wheezing began, and my lungs burned as I gasped for air. I tried to cough up something I knew wasn't there, and the pressure in my chest felt like an elephant was sitting on me. Panic built on panic. I couldn't tell whether the fear of losing everything was bringing on the attack or the attack was feeding the fear.

I was getting ready to lose everything I'd ever known. Everything I was used to. Everyone I depended on. My whole life as I knew it.

"Just settle down and breathe deeply. It will pass," Papa said, patting me on the back in case it was more stuck candy bar than asthma. "You haven't had an asthma attack in so long. I'd almost forgotten how bad they can be."

"I need you to be strong, Lou," Mama said. She held my hand and rubbed it like she was willing confidence into me. "Until this war is over, you kids are going to have to run this town."

My wheezing was under control by the time a deputy barged in and looked directly at Sheriff Gabe.

"Sir, we've got trouble. It's the Germans."

CHAPTER 4

Sheriff Gabe, Papa, Mama, Silver and I ran after the deputy. We kicked up a cloud of dust running across Main Street to the Cool Down Bar, the only place in town I was not allowed to go until I was sixteen. Not until that day. A black wooden chair flew out the door, followed by a lanky, tumbling tangle of an Italian rolling in the road and cussing up a blue streak. Mama marched over to him, placed one of her chunky heels on his chest and with hands on her hips thanked him *not* to curse in front of ladies. He glanced my way as his face turned splotchy shades of red and promised her in broken English not to curse again in front of *signores*.

A massive German in crimson suspenders and faded blue trousers ran out the door and down a couple of stairs, rolling up his sleeves en route. One glare from Mama stopped him in his tracks.

"Ma'am, you best get out of way," he said in a deep, gruff voice tinged with a German accent. His nostrils flared, and I swear I saw fire coming from his eyes. Silver leapt forward and growled at him, baring his teeth.

"You lay *one* finger on her, and it will be the *last* thing you do," Papa said from behind. The German turned back toward the bar to find the sheriff, the deputy and Papa leading out three more drunk Germans and one wobbly Italian in handcuffs.

"Now all of you, *sit*," Papa ordered.

The men reeked of beer that didn't survive the brawl. A few pieces of glass from what was left of several amber bottles nested in their straggly hair.

"Time to close down the German Bund here once and for all," Papa announced. "We will *not* tolerate fighting in our town. You are *not* welcome here anymore. The sheriff and deputy *will* escort you back to your resort. Pack your bags and be out of the county before sundown, or I *will* press charges for disturbing the peace and you *will all* go to jail."

The Germans called themselves the "German American Bund," or the "Bund" for short. They took up residence at one of the resorts in the backwoods of the mountains nearby a few months back. In school the week before, Aunt Mary had taught us about groups in America that were sympathetic to Hitler's reign, the Bund being one of the largest and most vocal. "You can't be too careful these days," she had said, "of the Germans *or* the Italians."

The Italians fighting in the bar were war prisoners that had arrived a few days before with some people from the state to do manual work along the lake. How so many violent people ended up in the middle of this God-forsaken, dot of existence in northern California without even one mile of railroad track to boot was beyond me.

War. War was coming to my town. War was in my home, in my head, in my lungs. I heard a scream rip through the tension hovering in the street. Everyone stared at the source of the scream. Me. The scene suffocated me, and I felt asthma waging war with my lungs for a second time that day. Even so, I belted out another scream, louder and fiercer than its predecessor. No one said a word. Even the birds hushed overhead.

My head shook violently. My hair filled my mouth, but nothing choked my words.

I turned and screamed directly at Papa. "What would we have done if all you men had already gone to war?" I yelled and pointed a quivering finger at Mama. "And all you were in Richmond?" My knees shook uncontrollably, and the tears stung my face. Sobs wracked my body, and nothing I did could stop the breakdown.

Mama ran over and held me as I collapsed in the street by the German who inched back, away from me. Panic mixed with fear and an unhealthy dose of adrenaline overpowered her hold, and I pushed away and rose to two shaky feet.

"This is a disaster!" I screamed as angst and anxiety propelled my skinny legs forward. The shaking feet beneath me started running on a path of their own design, out of town, then turned toward the lake. I tried to outrun what was to come like a rabbit tries to outrun a wolf. We both knew it was pointless, but we had to try.

I made it down to the lake, jumped in and swam. The water was cold, just the shock I needed. I needed to feel something, something familiar, some pain that was manageable. My clothes pulled against each stroke. My boots filled with water and threatened to drag me down. But the fear was too strong for drowning.

I made it to the island. Silver nearly caught up to me, leapt into my wake, and dogpaddled across. I ran to the other side of the island as fast as my shaking feet would take me and collapsed. A few seconds later, Silver sprawled beside me, his tongue lolling outside his mouth.

Curling up as close to fetal position as my lanky body allowed, I stared toward the west, rocking to and fro, the town and its troubles at my back. Mount Callisto loomed across the lake, daring me to scream at her. But my lungs won out. Frustrated and scared, I belted out the truth as I knew it.

"*There is no way on earth I can run this town!*" My words echoed across the lake, beyond the mountain to the far side of sanity.

CHAPTER 5

"Heavenly Father, protect these men as they leave to fight for this great nation. Hold them in the palm of Your hand, and bring them back safely to us. Watch over these women as they travel far and wide to work and support the country's war effort in this time of need. Care for these children left behind as they need every bit of your grace and mercy. In your Holy name we pray, Amen."

The circuit rider finished the prayer and the service ended with a solemn hymn. The congregation followed him silently out of the stale church into the cloudy, drizzly weather waiting outside. When I was a baby, Mama and Papa held church services in our cozy little living room. After about a year and a half of that, Claret Lake had grown so much that a freestanding church was needed to accommodate all the worshipers. So Papa and several other townsmen got together and built Claret Lake's first dedicated church out of stone from the quarry two counties over.

The seminary down near Napa sent a minister up to Lagune County every weekend to provide Sunday services. He traveled around the lake, giving services at four or five different towns in the area, spent the night at people's houses, and then went back down to Napa.

But that was most likely the last service for a while. The circuit rider was on his last tank of government-rationed gasoline, and by the time he got back down the mountains to Napa, his car would probably have to coast into town on nothing more than fumes.

"What's that rumbling noise?" I asked Papa. He raised a finger and pointed toward a bend in the dirt road. Four large buses rolled into town and lined up to change Claret Lake forever. They parked one after the other on the road outside the church. The first two blue buses had "Navy/San Francisco" emblazoned on signs hanging from strings tied to rusted-out windowsills. The two buses behind them had the words "Richmond Shipbuilders" painted on a sheet of what must have once been shiny silver metal.

I stood back from the crowd, stood in that space between loneliness and resentment. Around me, the women started crying, the kids began clinging, and the men tried to calm everyone down. I was so angry about what was happening that I didn't want to talk to anyone and crossed my arms in protest. A drop of rain plopped right on the middle of my head and trickled down past my left ear.

"You'll do just fine, Lou." Papa gave me a longer than normal hug. "You're stronger than you know."

I hugged him hard, willing him to stay, begging him to stay. But he let go, backed up and hugged Mama who looked like she was losing her best friend.

"Stay safe," she said, looking him straight in the eye, a tear escaping and running down her cheek. Papa wiped it away, nodded and lifted his duffle bag from the ground. He gave Silver a quick pat on the head and threw us a kiss as he boarded the bus.

"Last call for Lagune County," the men driving the first bus bellowed out. They each wore a dark blue piece of cloth with two yellow letters—SP—just above their elbows. "All aboard." With a lack of military precision, the rest of the men threw their packs on their backs and boarded the buses. When the last man's boots left the ground of Claret Lake, the wheels began to turn, churning up a cloud of dust over the road.

The women ran down the street after them, trying to grab one last touch from their menfolk through the open windows. Many fell short and lay prostrate in the street, their children running and screaming behind them. Most of the kids didn't understand why their parents had to go away, or why they were being left behind. With me.

"We need to get going, ladies," the round-spectacled shipyard representative announced timidly. He held a bullhorn up to his pursed lips and waved his free hand. "Ladies? Please? This is the last stop for this county." His expression changed from stern to concerned to exacerbated. The commotion must have been disconcerting to him, but maybe months of this exact scene jaded his conscience, and I only saw feigned worry. It was hard to tell.

The women stood up, their children clinging to them. Tears trailed down their dirt-stained cheeks as they hugged each child one last time, then let go and climbed aboard their link to survival.

"We'll look after 'em, Doc and me," Aunt Mary shouted out in her best schoolmarm voice, waving her ninety-year-old arm in a flimsy blouse that fluttered in the wind like a sail in the evening breeze before a storm.

"Look Lou, you've got to take care of everyone," Mama told me with one heel aboard the bus and one firmly on the ground. She gripped my shoulders and looked me straight in my teary, yet frustrated eyes. "You and Jimmy are the oldest ones left, well, except for Mary and Doc." She glanced to my left, then shook her head. "You've lived here all your life, and you know the ins and outs of the seasons. You may not know it yet, but you're strong. You're a survivor. Be sure to do all of your school work and remember to keep up your swimming.

Have one of the boys row beside you. You need to keep your asthma under control. It wouldn't be good to get pneumonia for a while."

"And Rex will watch over you in his own way," she added, glancing over my shoulder and nodding quickly. I turned to see the tribal leader standing beside the schoolhouse with his arms crossed. He told us to call him Rex because we could not easily pronounce his Indian name. He stood a foot taller than any man in town, his silver hair draping across both shoulders. Dusty Chuck Taylor's covered his feet, and he wore blue jeans rolled up mid-calf. Across his checked cotton shirt lay a neckpiece of clamshells and abalone shells. A somber expression remained on his face from when most of the tribal males boarded the military buses. At eighty-five, he, like Doc, was considered too old to be called up.

"All this will be over before you know it," Mama said. "I'll write when I can. Remember, I'm doing this because I love you."

She hugged me tightly one last time, and I broke down and hugged her back.

"I know, Mama. I'll do the best I can," I said.

"I love you," we said together. Those were the last words we both spoke and heard as the bus roared to life, coughing and sputtering, then chugged down the street.

Jimmy Hastings walked over, took my right hand and squeezed it as ten kids lined up beside us.

"Wave, Lou," he whispered into my ear. "We have to look strong for the kids. Take out your frustration on my hand," he offered. I did as he said and gave his hand a death grip, my rough nails digging deep into his rugged skin. Out of the corner of my eye I saw him wince, but he said nothing.

Six-year-old Becky Petitjohn clung to my leg like a newborn kitten to its mama and cried into my dirt-encrusted dungarees. I patted the child on the shoulder, my finger catching on her yellow gingham check pinafore. I had never realized what a tiny creature she was.

Aunt Mary and Doc wobbled over with their walking sticks and placed their feeble hands on Becky's tiny shoulders, shaking from sobs that wouldn't cease.

Silver sensed my frustration and set up camp by my feet. We watched the bus veer around the corner, out of town, and out of our lives.

"It'll be okay, Becky," I said, trying to believe it for myself. "It will all be okay."

Mind over matter, Lou. Mind over matter. I repeated the phrase over and over to myself, but deep inside, I didn't believe a word of it.

And I decided then and there I would *never* swim another day in my life.

CHAPTER 6

"Okay, everybody. Listen up," I said from the walnut pulpit in the front of the church. Silver staked out territory by my right foot. I cleared my throat like the circuit rider before he delivered God's word and leaned against the podium. Hopefully, God wouldn't mind my using his house for a non-church related meeting.

Jimmy climbed the ten stone stairs leading from the hand-carved wooden pews up to the pulpit and sat on the rug-covered step at my left.

Secretly, I'd been stuck on the tall, olive-skinned boy with tousled brown curls that flirted with his neck ever since he and his folks moved to town five years ago from somewhere in New Mexico. Jimmy was only a couple of years ahead of me, but he was almost as tall as Rex, which made him look older. Occasionally, he looked at me "that way," then shied away and started calling me Pipsqueak, a nickname I tolerated only because he was the one using it.

The younger kids occupied the wine-colored cushions on the front pew while the older kids straggled in and spaced themselves throughout the remaining pews, crossing their arms and whispering amongst each other. Aunt Mary and Doc sawed timbers in the back row and let out two large yawns. *Big help they're going to be.*

Clearing my throat, I launched into my role as newly appointed town leader.

"I made a list of the jobs we need to do to keep Claret Lake going while everyone is away. Jimmy's going to drive the school bus for us since he's the only one who knows how to drive, and we have almost a full tank of gasoline left in it. When the gas runs out, we'll all have to walk. School still meets five days a week but only until noon each day."

Moans and murmurs emanated from the middle rows.

"Now, everyone volunteer for whatever suits you best, and we'll fill in from there. We'll all have to share in each of the chores when we can. Other than that, Jimmy and I will step in whenever anyone has problems and pretty much help you all out."

"Who made you the boss of us?" Tommy Masters grumbled. Tommy was twelve going on two, and still pitched fits like a toddler. I knew his anger, like mine, stemmed from his parents going away, but his grumbling annoyed me.

"Would you like to be in charge instead?" I asked, offering him my notepaper and pencil.

Tommy shook his head, crossed his arms, and flopped back down on one of the handmade cushions Mama made for the church pews to make them more comfortable during the second circuit rider's infamous long sermons. Tommy's anger flared in his eyes.

"I understand you're angry, Tommy," I said. "My papa should be here, too, not off fighting in some God-forsaken corner of the world." I glanced up behind me at the cross over the baptistery and sent up a quick repentance. "No offense, God."

I turned back to the hostile room and looked around. "Would anyone else like to be in charge?" I asked, looking at the cheerless faces only partially filling the holy room.

Silence.

"Alrighty then. Let's get this town organized. Aunt Mary's in charge of teaching school and Doc's the one taking care of medical problems. I hope." Glancing toward the two geriatrics at the rear of the church, I heaved a deep sigh, shook my head and returned my tired eyes to the paper clutched in my hands.

"Here's the list of chores. Hunting for fresh meat. Fishing for, well, fish. Cooking our daily meals. Cleaning up after the cooking. Doing the laundry. Running the grocery store and the restaurant. Taking care of the post office and the mail. Manning the pump house. Taking care of the horses. Managing the airport. Tending the fields. Managing the school office. Running the school library. Harvesting the grapes, walnuts and pears come fall. Working in the hayfields. Anyone?"

Silence again.

"Look, I'm not keen on doing all this alone. Bev, Julie, Fern, Barbara?" Bev Edwards and Julie Finch were twelve, and Fern and Barbara Dawson trailed them by just a year. The fidgety girls fiddled with their long blonde curls. "What would you like to do?"

"Go to the beach, play in the surf, and meet some dreamy guys," Bev said. The rest of them nodded in agreement, curls bouncing around their smiling faces, looking heavenward as if asking the Good Lord to answer their prayers.

Bev, Julie, Fern and Barbara hung out a lot after school. It seemed every group had a name. They were called the Flashy Four, mostly because they cared more about the latest city fashions than anything else. Their parents traveled between Claret Lake and San Francisco and habitually brought back magazines touting the latest fashions. When I had time after work and my chores to hang out with them, we were called the Flashy Five, although I was happy with my non-flashy, flying-friendly clothes.

"Why don't you just open your eyes and see the handsome hunks you have right outside your front door?" Clayton Carpenter piped up. He, his brother Murph, and Jimmy hooted and hollered. Clayton was born shortly after me and was my oldest and best friend since the first grade. Everyone called him Clay. His younger brother Murphy, or Murph, arrived on the scene ten months to the day after Clay.

The little kids clapped and laughed. At least spirits seemed to be getting a bit better.

"I need some help here," I growled. "Look, I'll manage the airport, run the school office, the school library, and the pump house at the lake, but I can't do everything on my own."

"Oh, it looks like you're doing a pretty good job to me," Ralph Oglesbee said. "You're putting us all out of a job." Ralph's red hair stood out against the stark white paint and brown oak pews of the sanctuary.

"Just for that, you're in charge of hunting."

"Oh man, I just *hate* being outdoors and running wild in the forest." Ralph rolled his eyes, flailed his arms in the air over his bushy head, and chuckled what bordered on a sinister laugh. "Pure punishment for me," he said, clasping his hands to his chest, his head falling backward.

"Fine," I said. "Just make sure we have some meat that we can put up in the icebox for winter. We have to stock up early. Okay, how about someone for fishing?"

"I'll tease the trout," Clay said, raising his long, lean fingers in the air and wiggling them.

Relieved that someone actually volunteered, I gave him a smile and a quick bow. "Thanks, Clay. You can use Papa's boat and fishing tackle if you want to."

"Now, Sheriff Gabe handed me this letter before he shipped out." I pulled a single sheet of paper out of a long, narrow envelope, laid it down on the pulpit, and smoothed out the creases. "According to this, the Ground Observer Corps of the Aircraft Warning Service needs a Chief Volunteer Aircraft Observer to look for enemy aircraft from the forest ranger's tower just south of town. So, who's up for a little aircraft spotting?"

Quiet fell over the room, and everyone looked down like there was something interesting in each lap. I knew the reason, but I couldn't say anything just yet. The fear of seeing an enemy plane would scare the trousers off of just about any of us. It's enough that the emissaries' plane continued to call our dock home, even after almost a year.

"How 'bout you do dat," little Becky squeaked from the second pew. "You wike pwanes."

"You're right, Becky. Perfect. I'll be the Chief Volunteer Aircraft Observer," I said, giving her a nod.

The youngest child left behind, Becky was Eddie Petitjohn's baby sister.

"I'll help with the tower watch," Eddie said, sitting upright in the pew, holding Becky's tiny little hand. "It's near my house, and I can see Becky play from up there." Eddie spent most of his time watching after Becky and playing with fire. "I can build fires for whoever needs it, too, you know, for cooking and all and when winter comes."

I nodded in approval, thanked him and continued. "I know it's a while away, but when it's time to harvest the walnuts, grapes and pears, I'm going to need all hands on deck. It will take each of us working every day together to get those crops in. Most of us have had at least a little experience in the fields on the slopes of Mount Callisto, so if you have questions when the time comes, just ask. Same goes for haying season. Everything else will just have to go on the back burner during that time, including school, or else we're going to be left with nothing to sharpen our teeth on come winter. So, tending the fields. It's important because if we want to eat, we have to have crops to harvest, right?"

"I'll give it a whack," Murph said.

"I'll do that, too," Tommy offered. The two volunteers shook hands.

"And we'll handle the post office and take care of the horses," Barbara and Fern offered. The eleven-year-old Dawson twins dressed alike, but their personalities differed like night and day, Barbara being a nature girl and Fern preferring organizing and being indoors.

"Bev and Julie, would you please handle the restaurant and grocery store? The cooking and baking? We all have to eat. We won't be charging for any of the food or the supplies, but we need someone to make sure we all have three meals a day and that the supplies are doled out. I'll leave the Café and grocery unlocked, and you can use whatever you want."

"Sure, whatever," they said, filing their nails to what must have been nubs. Just two years behind me in school, Bev and Julie would rather fall into a vat of slithering snakes than do any actual work.

I knew I should have been in charge of feeding everyone since I had worked in the restaurant for Mama and Papa, but with the other chores I needed to take on, Bev and her bosom buddy were just going to have to be in charge of the cooking. I hoped there were some recipes hidden in the pages of those fashion magazines somewhere.

"Teaching school is supposed to be handled by Aunt Mary, but I'm not sure how that is going to work out," I sighed, watching her drool slightly while she dozed on the back row, her head resting on Doc's bony shoulder. She wasn't technically anyone's aunt, but she was Mama's best friend and that's what she called her, and so did the rest of us.

"And if anyone gets sick, Doc can handle that, I expect." Everyone turned around to see his head fall back and hit the stone wall. He let out a snore. Giggles erupted from every side of the room.

"Hopefully no one gets sick," Ralph snickered.

We decided the girls should live in town with me, and the boys should set up camp at Jimmy's place just south of town. That way he and I could keep an eye on everyone, at least at night.

Becky raised her little hand and shook it wildly in the air. "What about me, Miss Lou?"

"Well now, let me think," I said, scratching my head. "How about you help Fern and Barbara feed the horses, and you can help me straighten up the house each day."

"Swell!" she exclaimed, grabbing Eddie's hands and bouncing in the pew.

CHAPTER 7

"Ninety-one, ninety-two, ninety-three, ninety-four." I counted out loud as I climbed up, my feet memorizing the rungs on the forestry tower ladder. "My first day as Chief Volunteer Aircraft Observer." I looked down at Silver whining on the ground below.

"If nothing else, I'll get plenty of exercise in this mission," I yelled down. I liked to call it a mission since it felt like I was helping out with the war, helping to bring Mama and Papa home sooner.

I took the early morning, midday, and evening shifts so that Eddie could watch over little Becky during the day. Sometimes I stayed all night. Better that than have the enemy invade while everyone was asleep. I planned to catch a few catnaps during the time Eddie was on watch to keep from falling asleep on duty.

When I climbed past the ninety-fourth rung of the ladder, I stepped into my new home away from home. The lone tower perched high in the sky, nestled between valley oaks, Douglas firs, and lofty Ponderosa pines. The dark-green wooden structure blended perfectly with the surrounding foliage. It creaked and swayed gently as the southerly winds whistled and swirled through the forest.

Years ago, it was constructed as a forest ranger tower to spot forest fires. But the war changed a lot of things, and fire spotting went on the back burner. A square area about eight feet by eight feet sat like a roosters nest at the top and was covered with a slanted roof also made of wood and painted the same deep green as the rest of the tower. The stale stench of mold crept up from the damp baseboards. No glass windows adorned the room, only large rectangular gaps open to the elements and the summer breeze, complete with a nice view of the surrounding valleys and mountains. Mount Callisto kept me company to the northwest, and several hilly ranges extended to the east.

A creek that began at the lake due north of the tower trickled nearby, carrying schools of fish gliding by beneath me every hour or so. Crickets sang in the willows that dangled their branches close to the creek, and birds hopped to the edge to grab a cool drink of crisp mountain water every few minutes. The bright candy apple red cardinals were my favorite birds to visit since they supposedly brought good luck. At that point, we needed all the luck we could get.

Exploring the contents of my "hut on stilts," I found a grayish-colored government-issue aluminum desk complete with field glasses, paper, pencils, a rotary pencil sharpener attached to one end, and a chair with a drab green plastic cushion, thank goodness. Bev and Julie would have pitched a fit about the color scheme—not fashionable at all. A dim lamp graced the left-hand corner of the desk, and I flipped the switch on to test it.

"Looks like the electricity still works up here," I said. I shimmied out of the pack I hauled up on my back and dumped the contents on the desk. Pulling my papa's favorite all-purpose knife out of the front pocket of my soft, worn dungarees, I sliced through a thick wad of tape to open a box that arrived the day before at the post office, addressed to the Chief Volunteer Aircraft Observer, namely, me. Eddie had been kind enough to haul it up the ninety-four rungs earlier that morning. Flipping back the cardboard flaps, a document titled "War Department—Signal Corps Field Manual—Aircraft Warning Service" stared me in the face. It held instructions for the tower's new mission.

"No lack of reading material here," I said, flipping through its hundred or so pages and tossing it to the side. Underneath it were drawing after drawing of airplanes used in wartime, or "war birds" as Papa called them, and drawing after drawing of various enemy aircraft. A log book was supplied for documenting aircraft sightings along with instructions on how to contact the nearest filter center, which for me was Hamilton Army Air Field. If I ever saw a plane, I was

43

instructed to immediately contact them and say "Army Flash." That meant I had spotted a plane. Hunting through the two remaining desk drawers, I found a radio and set out to change it to Hamilton's frequency. *No time like the present to get started.*

"Testing. Testing. Over," I muttered, pushing several buttons in sequence until I finally made out Hamilton Field through the static. Silver heard my voice and responded below with a bark and a whimper. I grabbed hold of the wooden slats on the side of the tower and glanced over the side to see him wagging his tail in earnest below.

"I'll have to rig a way to get you up here with me one of these days, boy," I said. "Maybe you'll fit in my pack if we squeeze you in. We'll give it a try next time. Just sit tight for now and guard the base of the tower for me, okay?"

He gave a quick bark, turned around three times in a circle, sniffed the air to the left and then to the right, and finally laid down by the ladder, head up, eyes alert for danger.

Back to the task at hand, I studied the papers and drawings, starting to learn the shapes of the Japanese and American planes. At first, many looked alike, but as the day wore on, I began to notice the subtle and not so subtle differences more clearly.

44

I held up the last page of enemy aircraft in my hand, stood, and glanced north toward the lake. Looking back and forth, I shook my head.

"Couldn't miss that one in a million years," I said.

The silhouette I held was the spitting image of the emissaries' plane.

CHAPTER 8

July 1942

"How long do you suppose that plane's gonna sit there?" Clay asked, digging his fingers around in the moist dirt by the lake. He pulled a long, thin squirming worm from its home and baited his hook.

"Who knows," I said. "It is kind of eerie to see it sitting there day after day, month after month, knowing it belongs to the enemy."

"Well, I say 'finder's keepers,'" Clay said, tossing his fishing line as far as it would reach into the lake. The worm splashed when it hit the water, then sank out of sight. "Come on little fishes. Grab that nice fresh tasty worm."

"Hope you catch something—I'm starving. Guess I'd better get to the wash," I said, rolling my eyes and tossing a bar of soap in the air. "One of these days the girls are going to have to pitch in and help with this."

"At least you have me and Silver to keep you company," Clay said. He grinned at me, then turned back to watch his pole dance over the water as a fish played with the worm.

I grabbed the bar of soap and a mud-stained shirt from the pile of dirty clothes and waded out into the lake. Silver laid down on the dock to watch me, his paws flopping over the edge.

Washing the clothes took longer than I thought. Mama used to clean all of our clothes—before she went away. While she scrubbed, I would play in the lake and toss a ball to Silver. Thanks to the war, I would never take this grueling task for granted again.

Thankfully, Mama had stocked up on Ivory soap. I watched the bar float nearby as I wrung the last of the water from the shirt, laid it in the basket set aside for clean clothes, and grabbed a pair of dungarees from the dirty pile.

"These must be Eddie's. They smell like smoke."

"I've never known someone to like playing with fire as much as he does," Clay said. "Hot dog! I've got a bite!" He ran backward toward the yard, pulling his pole and a floundering trout with him. Silver ran after the duo, barking and swatting at the fish.

The poor trout gasped, flailed and fought to get back into the water, but it was no match for Clay. I knew how the fish felt—understood the feeling of not being able to catch your breath, knowing you're going to die if you don't get air, or in the fish's case, water. It flapped its silvery body back and forth, the slapping sound slowing the longer it was kept from the water. Turning my back on the fight and plight of the fish we would be eating for dinner, I tossed the dungarees aside, reached down to grab the soggy shirt I had just washed, and walked toward the clothesline by the house. Taking a couple of clothespins from Mama's wash-day tule basket, I clipped the shirt to the thin line to dry in the summer breeze.

"That's a looker," Clay said, proudly holding up his morning catch. "Bev should be able to feed all of us with this one. Looks like they're biting today. Must be the juicy worms." He held up the next wriggling victim and shook it in my face before baiting his hook a second time.

I went back down to the lake to finish the wash. I rubbed, scrubbed and removed most of the dirt and stains from the last piece of clothing and hung it on the line. The day's wash fluttered in the breeze, and the scent of fresh laundry drifted toward the lake. Wading back into the water, I rinsed the dirt and grass from my feet, then pulled myself up onto the dock next to Silver and Clay. Out of the corner of my eye, the plane beckoned me.

"I've been thinking about what you said—about 'finder's keepers' and all. Do you really think so, Clay?"

He nodded his head and grinned. "You should look inside the plane and see if there's anything we can use."

"Maybe just a peek," I said, curious about the secrets the plane held behind its canopies. I shook the remnants of water from my feet and gave Silver a pat.

The plane sat high off the water near the end of the dock. The wind blew across the lake, and small waves lapped against the pontoons, making the plane bob up and down like a buoy. Grabbing onto the trailing edge of the wing, I stepped onto the metal pontoon. My weight made it sink a few inches into the lake until water covered my toes. I pulled myself up onto the wing by the fuselage and scraped my knee on an exposed rivet. A few drops of blood dripped onto the wing. Turning to sit on the warm metal, I applied pressure to my wound until it started to scab. I stood up on the wing, leaned over the first of the dirt-streaked canopies, and peered inside.

"What do you see?" Clay asked.

"Nothing yet. It's covered in grime." I ran my hand along the edge and felt for a latch or a handle. Toward the back of the pilot's canopy, I found what I was looking for. I pulled the latch toward the front of the plane and tried to pull the glass back.

"It's stuck."

"Maybe there's a latch on the other side, too," Clay said.

"You know, you may be right." I crawled over the top of the plane, straddling it like a horse.

"Now all I need is a lasso, a cowboy hat, and my bolt-action and I'll be Annie Oakley."

Clay turned, slapped his knee and laughed as I sat astride the top of the airplane like a cowboy riding a bronc. I slid down the other side and found a second latch. The canopy slid back, and I had my first glimpse into the world of the enemy.

The stale stench of mold and sunbaked leather filled the cockpit. I looked around and was surprised at the amount of space in the cockpit compared to the tandems I'd flown in before the war.

Clay whooped and hollered outside. "I got another bite. It's bigger than the last one." I glanced up and saw a huge fish fighting a losing battle with the end of the fishing line. I turned back to the cockpit, trying to determine the best way to get into it.

Stepping down, my bare feet found the gray leather to be warm and stiff. Wishing it hadn't been so long since I'd been in a plane, I slid into the pilot's domain. A puff of dust rose out of cracks in the seat and caused me to sneeze—twice. Sniffling, I rubbed my nose and surveyed my surroundings. Everything was gray or black. The lettering on the instrument panel must have once been painted white, but it was chipped and yellowed with age. All the labels were in Japanese because I couldn't read a word of it. But as different as the plane was from the ones I had been in before the war, many of the instruments looked vaguely familiar.

"Do you think you could fly this thing?" Clay asked, jumping onto the pontoon and climbing up on the wing.

"No idea. Everything's written in gibberish, but I do recognize several of the instruments."

He peered over my shoulder into the cockpit. "It looks pretty empty to me—just a seat, some dials, and the smell of the enemy. Let me know if you find anything interesting we can use. I gotta take those fish over to Bev before they bake in the sun."

He shimmied down the wing and leapt onto the dock. Grabbing his catch-of-the-day, he headed for town.

Now, let's see what treasures you're hiding in here, I thought, focusing on the contents of the cockpit. A few papers peeked out of a pocket attached to the side of the plane by my leg. I grabbed them and scanned the pages. *There's no way I can read this.*

I placed my feet on the rudder pedals in the floorboard and pushed. They were mushy, but they moved. Glancing behind me, I saw the rudder waggle back and forth.

The leather seat squeaked as I sat back up and folded my fingers around the stick protruding between my knees. Grasping it, I pulled it to the left, then to the right. Forward, then back. Surprisingly, after all the time the plane had been sitting there locked up, the stick moved easily, but it squealed when I shifted it.

Maybe it needs oil, I thought. Studying where the noise could have come from, I heard it squeal again. It sounded like a human.

"Lou! You got a letter!"

My head jerked up and I saw Fern running down to the dock.

"It's from your mama!" she shouted.

I scrambled out of the cockpit and crawled onto the wing. I slid the canopy closed and lowered myself onto the pontoon. Grabbing Fern's outstretched hand, I hopped onto the dock, the shift in weight making the plane bob again, creating waves that broke over the shore.

Fern pressed the envelope into my hand. "Maybe the war's over! Maybe they're all coming home!" She rubbed her hands together and crossed her arms, tapping her shoe on the dock, eager to hear the contents of the letter.

"Sure hope so," I said, ripping open the thin envelope. I withdrew a single sheet of paper, unfolded it, and read the words to Fern and Silver.

Dear Lou,

    I know it's been a while since we all had to leave, and I haven't written you but this once. For that I am truly sorry. We work so many hours here at the shipyard that by the time we're finished for the day, we collapse into the stiff cots they pass off as beds. They call us 'Rosie the Riveters' and "Wendy the Welders' and have us making the biggest, best ships in the world for our soldiers. We can't help but win the war with the fine ships we're sending out!

    I got one letter from your papa. He is in France and is worried about us both, but I've written him to tell him we're doing fine. I just hope my letter finds him overseas.

    How are things in Claret Lake? Is everyone getting along? Everyone doing their chores and schoolwork? There should still be plenty of food left in the store. We tried to stock up for you and the kids before we had to leave. I know you're handling things just like I would. I know you have everything under control.

    I hate that I'm here and you're there. All the mamas want you to say hello to the kids for them. Make sure to do your swimming, Lou.

    Love you,
    Mama

My spirits folded like the letter as I stuffed it back into the envelope and handed it to Fern.

"They're not coming home," I said, turning toward the house before Fern could see my frustration breach the dam I had erected to hold back my tears.

"At least you got a letter," Fern mumbled from behind. I turned to see her shuffling back toward town, head down, kicking rocks out of the dirt along the way.

Passing by the clothesline, I felt a pair of dungarees to see if they were dry.

Still wet. Just like the tears that finally broke through.

CHAPTER 9

September, 1942

After three months, everyone except Aunt Mary and Doc seemed perpetually mopey. The kids did what they could, but completing the day to day chores occupied a great deal of time. Instead of getting mail every couple of days, it slid to once every couple of weeks. Barbara brought out the outdoorsy Fern we never knew existed, and together they rode the chestnut horses more than they handled the post office business. Tommy and Murph played hide and seek in the fields more than they tended them, and more often than not, they fell asleep during the game, waking up only to Bev's ringing of the bell for supper.

Bev and Julie seemed to be working harder than anyone, which surprised Jimmy and me. Bev mostly cooked, and Julie shifted to baking. It seemed those fashion magazine writers contributed a good number of recipes along with advice that the way to a man's heart was through his stomach. No complaints from anyone about the food, least not from the boys, so it must have worked.

Every night the girls provided us with a feast, and every morning, leftovers. Clay kept Bev stocked with fish from the lake. The fish bit more some weeks than others, but when they did bite, we all piled into the restaurant to make sure not a morsel went to waste.

Eddie constructed and tended a fire every evening at my house and at Jimmy's for warmth, whether we needed it or not. Other than that, he relieved me in the watchtower every four hours or so. Since I was technically in charge of it, I spent more time up there. But having someone to take over for a bit relieved me of some of the stress that had built up over the past few months.

Jimmy spent a lot of time with the younger kids and helped them with their chores. When he came around, they did great work, but as soon as the cat was away, the mice would play. And play, they did, in abundance. It felt wrong to interrupt their fun—they were children after all. But if the fun continued and the chores played second fiddle for much longer, trouble would not evade us for long.

I heard Jimmy toot the school bus horn outside the front door. The girls sauntered out, shuffling their feet in the dirt and climbed aboard. He motioned for me to come out, but I waved him on. He delivered a quick salute and drove away, smoke billowing out of the grumpy old bus. I took a deep breath, turned and sat on the divan, running my fingers through Silver's soft fur.

It was time for school, and I knew Aunt Mary would chide me for playing hooky, but after being at the lookout tower almost all night and returning to straighten the mess the girls made that morning throughout the house, I deserved a break.

I looked around the home Papa built when he and Mama moved to Claret Lake in 1924. Rising to my weary feet, I peddled around the familiar room and ran my fingers along the cold, rough stone that Papa used to rock over the split pine log house interior a decade after he built the place. That addition made the walls about two feet thick, so the house stayed toasty warm in the winter and crispy cool in the summer.

On the inside, he laid black cement in between the lava rocks that Mount Callisto must have left as a present around the shores of the lake years ago. Along with the black cement, he mixed in and decorated it with Indian arrowheads, California diamonds, and Indian beads. Two alcoves adorned the top of the stone chimney standing sentinel in the main room like a four-star general.

"I wonder if there will ever be a five-star general," I muttered. Silver looked up and flapped his tail against the divan.

In the early days of Claret Lake, ours was the only residence in town. The other houses mostly nestled among the trees down the road a piece to the south. Our house sat on a slight hill by the lake, and our dock resided at the end of the stone wall Papa built between our house and the lake. When the town's water needs rose, he put in a pumping station on the island just off the end of the dock. The water required 'straining and draining' before it made the trip uphill to the water tower the town installed. Mama volunteered for that and became the town's one-woman water department. I watched and learned to do it practically blindfolded.

Technically and legally the island belonged to us, but the local Indian tribe believed it was sacred ground. Even though Papa allowed them to hunt on it, they made us members of their tribe so that a tribal family would own it. Papa would have let them hunt there regardless, but having us as members meant a lot to the tribe, so we completed the ceremony. I remembered it vividly, like it happened yesterday.

I closed the wooden-slat screen door outside the kitchen behind Silver and me, turned, and bumped right into Rex. His strong, weathered hands grabbed my shoulders and kept me from falling.

"Okay, Little One?" he questioned in his deep voice. A sack full of quivers rested on his back, and he shifted his bow from his right hand to his left. The shells on his neckpiece clinked together, sounding like wind chimes on a breezy afternoon.

"I think so," I said. "We manage okay, but it's harder than I thought. I just hope we make it through this coming winter."

"Yes." He said the one simple word, and I smiled. I learned that was typically the bulk of his entire conversation with me. He nodded, turned and walked north about thirty paces, then stopped mid-stride. I watched as his form stood tall, stretching out his bow and retrieving an arrow. An unfortunate deer would not return home. I hoped Ralph would get better at hunting. We all craved fresh meat. Maybe Rex could teach him a thing or two about how to hunt. The tribe's ways were so different from ours, but they knew the land and nature better than any of us ever would.

I shrugged my shoulders and trudged through the sea of orange and yellow leaves starting to cover the ground.

Time for some island time, I thought. *Some alone time. Time away from life as I now know it—life as it began when those buses rolled out of town.*

Silver and my favorite book of all time, *Jean & Co., Unlimited,* accompanied me to my escape from the world on my day of playing hooky. The clear lake water was low, so we could walk over the short muddy isthmus connecting the dock to the island.

I loved to read, but since Claret Lake didn't have a town library, just the little one at school that was limited to school books, we had to buy any other books we wanted to read by mail. This one cost a dollar from the Junior Literary Guild, the place that sold books to us. They offered a "Junior Book of the Month Club." All the books arrived brand new with that special new book scent. I could close my eyes and smell the promise of adventure waiting beneath each cover and hardback edition. Mama and Papa couldn't afford a book every month for me, so I got one every other month. Six books a year. They'd given me a membership for my birthday for five years running.

"Lucky for me, my membership renewed recently," I said to Silver who frolicked in the leaves and chased a bug darting between a few fallen branches. "And lucky for me I found that money hidden deep behind the towels in the drawer next to the sink and sent it to the Guild. I probably should have saved it, though, because I bet funds for anything but survival prove scarce for a while."

Silver trotted over and licked my fingers. I patted his head. I knew he agreed with me. He always did.

I leaned back against my favorite old oak tree, its gnarled trunk and wide branches welcoming me. Pulling my legs in close, I realized my knobby knees almost reached my chin. I wrapped my sweater around them as a chill filled the air billowing off the lake. Pieces of tree bark flaked off around me and landed quietly in the leaves covering the last of the exposed brown dirt.

I closed my eyes for a moment and took in the crisp smell of the lake. A moth floated by and lighted on my nose. I flicked it off without thinking, hoping it wasn't hurt. How nice to be able to flit around from place to place, landing at one spot to rest, and at another to observe. Mama always said I must have had gypsy blood in me, always wanting to travel and explore. Right about then, I'd rather have been anywhere but where I was. Maybe it was more because of the war, or how Mama and Papa were taken from me, but I'd have rather been anywhere, *anywhere*, but there.

A sigh escaped my lips as I gently opened the first page and escaped into the book's adventure. The story centered around a girl of fourteen named Jean. She was American but traveled overseas to Europe for two years while her father worked a job in Russia and her mother traveled Europe to write a book. Jean attended school at a convent in France where she promptly met a number of "Jeans" from around the world—Jeanette from France, Giovanna from Italy, Janesika from Prague, Ioannachka from Russia, and Jovanka from Yugoslavia. They formed a group called "Jean & Company," and after the school year came to a close, they met each other throughout travels all over Europe. When they couldn't be together, they started a "Round Robin," a letter that traveled from one Jean to the next. Each would write of her adventures and send it on. Neither geographic nor language barriers kept the Jeans from their fabulous adventures.

Page one began my travel into her world and away from mine. Jean packed her steamer trunk for her first trip to Europe, and I imagined how it might feel to sail away on the high seas and beyond. The exuberance. The excitement. The anticipation. *Oh, what a lucky girl!*

Within an hour, I traveled from school in France to Christmas in Switzerland replete with mountain chalets, toboggans, and a million twinkling lights reflecting off of a recent winter snowfall. I turned the pages that had yellowed a bit and were dog-eared from years of reading, but they still filled a longing within me.

A flash of light brought me back to the present. I glanced up and looked across the shimmering water toward Mount Callisto.

"Is that Ralph and Tommy?" I asked Silver, reaching over to pat his head. Two figures climbed the steep slopes. "Ralph must be turning thirteen today." Climbing Mount Callisto on your thirteenth birthday was a rite of passage.

"Well, good for them," I said. "I'm not a bit upset they're playing hooky, too. Aunt Mary's schoolhouse must be pretty empty today."

Turning the adventure-laden pages with one hand, I stroked Silvers thickening winter fur with the other as I leapt back into Jean's world and escaped from what had become of mine.

CHAPTER 10

"Sleeping on the job, Eddie?" I said, peering into the tower from the top rung of the ladder.

"Lou, geez, you scared me. I must've fallen asleep."

"Why don't you go home and get some shut-eye," I said, hopping over the ledge. I shivered as the crisp fall breeze whipped through the tower.

"Don't mind if I do." Eddie gave me a quick salute, scampered down the ladder, and jogged toward his second nap of the morning.

Silver lounged in a patch of sunlight that crept through the swaying branches overhead and landed by the gurgling creek. He looked so comfortable, so unaware of what we kids were having to go through to keep the town in working order. Sometimes all I felt was sorry—sorry for myself. I would climb up in the tower and wallow in self-pity, wishing things could go back to how they used to be—when I hadn't a care in the world. When Mama and Papa took care of me instead of me taking care of this town. When all I had to complain about was a forced morning swim.

"Miss Lou! Miss Lou! You up there?" A squeaky voice and the sound of feet running through crunchy leaves interrupted my pity party.

Peering over the edge, I saw Becky running and jumping up and down like a bird trying to land on a porcupine.

"Becky, what are you doing down there?"

"I got a letter, Miss Lou! It has a big "V" on it!" She waved a small envelope over her head. "It came this morning to the post office. Miss Fern asked me to run it over for Eddie to read, but he's sound asleep and I can't get him to wake up, so I ran fast as a jackrabbit to see if you'd read it to me!"

I climbed down the ladder, took her hand in mine, and wiped a blanket of leaves off a large rock with the other so her gingham dress wouldn't get mussed. Silver trotted over and curled up in a sliver of sun that lit the ground near Becky's feet.

"Let's see what we have here, Miss Becky," I said, taking the letter from her outstretched hand and examining the cream-colored envelope. The red letters looked official, and the place where the stamp should be said *Free*.

"What's that "V" mean?"

"That means its V-mail. The V stands for Victory, so it's actually called 'Victory mail.'"

"Does that mean we won the war?"

"Not exactly, but it is mail that comes from the soldiers—our papas and grandpas and uncles and brothers who are fighting in the war."

"Oh! Is that from my daddy?"

"Let's open it and see."

Becky fidgeted and pulled on her fingertips, eager to see who had written the letter. I took care not to rip the paper so that I wouldn't mess up the lettering written inside. I had only seen one V-mail before this one. Papa sent a short note to me a couple of months back saying that he wouldn't be able to write for a while given that he was going behind enemy lines and it was so dangerous out there. He said he was in a remote town in France but that it wasn't nearly as remote as Claret Lake. He also said these new V-mail envelopes saved a lot of money for the post office, being that you wrote on the inside of the envelope instead of on a separate piece of paper. Funny how he was in the thick of the fighting and interested in how the post office saved money. I prayed every day that he would be kept safe, but I hadn't heard a word since.

"Why is the paper so tiny?" Becky asked.

Looking at the letter, it did look unusually small.

Smoothing out the opened envelope, I flipped it over and began reading to the eager little girl sitting beside me.

My dearest Eddie and Becky,

I hope you two are having a good time with Miss Lou and Mr. Jimmy and are behaving yourselves.

"We behavin' okay, Miss Lou?"

"You certainly are. Both you and Eddie are model citizens."

A smile bloomed across her face, and she looked back toward the letter.

I'm in a country called France. It's across the big Atlantic Ocean. The people here talk in a funny language with a strange accent. Sometimes it's hard to understand them, but I muddle through. It's a pretty place, lots of long grasses, rolling hills and winding stone walls like the one behind Miss Lou's house.

I'm staying in a stone cabin for a few days, less than half the size of our house back in Claret Lake. There is a small pond in the back where the owners let us fish when it's safe to be outside. I am trying to be brave for you. Be brave for me, too, 'ya hear? And be brave for your mama.

I miss you all so. I love you more than the sun on a chilly day, more than a present on Christmas morn! I don't know how long this will take to get to you, but hopefully it's before your birthday, Becky! Now you go get a big handful of candy from the grocery store for your birthday, and tell Miss Lou to charge it to me. Just make sure not to eat it all at once lest you get a tummy ache!

Now I gotta go catch some fish for dinner!

Love you both,

Papa

"I gotta go get my birthday candy! Hope there's some left—Miss Bev says we're starting to run low on food."

Becky headed toward town, skipping and singing. I glanced down at the letter in my hand. There was more.

Eddie, the rest of this letter is for you. Please don't read this to Becky. You are nearly fourteen—close to being a man—so I think you can handle this. The war is very hard and terribly scary. Bombs land all around us every day and every night. The bombs blast louder than ten thousand firecrackers and ruin the land for miles. The heat from the blasts could fry a crow in flight. I never knew war could be so terrifying—so real.

I know I'm your daddy, but I have to tell you, I'm scared. All day. All night. I want to get back to the two of you and your mama so badly, but if I don't make it back, please be there for Becky. She's such a little thing and needs a good man—a good brother—in her life to help her while she's growing up. Please promise me you'll take care of her. I love you both more than you'll ever know. The enemy gets closer by the minute. Hope this arrives to you safely.

All my love,
Papa

Tears crept down my cheeks, and hurt filled every crevice of my heart for our papas, our soldiers, and for those of us left behind. Folding the letter, I pressed the seal together and placed the paper in my pocket. I gave Silver a couple of pats on the head, climbed the ninety-four rungs back to the top of the tower, and looked out over the valley to the mountains in the distance. At least we were safe here. At least we didn't have the enemy bearing down on us every hour of every day.

I pulled the letter from my pocket and laid it on the desk, placing a corner of it under the lamp so it wouldn't blow away. When Eddie took over watch in a couple of hours, he would be able to read it without Becky around. He would have a place to scream. A place to cry. A place to be afraid. Maybe it's best Papa didn't write me. It was one thing to read about it from Eddie and Becky's papa, but it would be another to hear that kind of fear in my own papa's words.

A buzz droned in the distance, breaking the stillness of the morning. The sound reminded me of bees congregating at a hive or locusts invading the valley. Looking every direction for the source of the commotion, I only saw hawks and sparrows retreating into the trees. I grabbed the field glasses and scanned the sky. The noise grew louder and closer, becoming a roar that threatened to rip the heavens apart.

What on earth can that be?

The ground began to tremble and threatened to shatter the tower into a million pieces. Bracing myself in a corner, fear filled me, and I fought to keep my eyes open. My body shuddered as the air shook. When I thought the wooden structure could take no more, the wind turned violent. It blew through the tower with the force of a hundred tornados and brought with it the deafening roar of a thousand locomotives.

If that's an earthquake, I'm not safe up here!

But within the time between two heartbeats, I knew exactly what it was. A chill ran through my body, like a soul departing to the hereafter, and asthma took advantage of my plight.

A war plane was headed straight for Claret Lake.

CHAPTER 11

"Ham—Field—come—in—over." I clenched my chest with one hand, rummaging through the drawings in the desk drawers with the other as panic fueled my asthma attack. I tried desperately to locate what kind of plane nearly crashed into the tower.

Breathe, Lou. Breathe. Calm down and breathe. My heart raced and my palms were covered with sweat. I struggled to push air into my lungs, but it felt like I was breathing through a clogged straw. Asthma robbed me of every ounce of energy. Holding the radio, I fell to the floor, wheezing, and felt death toying with me.

"...there...Ham...Fie...ov..." Static pierced through the radio waves as my body went numb.

Mind over matter, Lou. Just get the words out.

I pushed the transmit button and gave all the strength I could muster.

"Claret—Lake—Army—Flash—over." I spoke each word as wholly as my lungs would allow. Pulling myself up into the chair, I laid my head on the cluttered desk.

Breathe in. Breathe out. Breathe in. Breathe out. In. Out. In. Out.

I felt a hand touch my back and begin to rub gentle circles. The rhythm made me want to go to sleep and free myself from the torture in my throat and lungs forever.

"Just relax, Lou," Jimmy said. "I'm here now. Close your eyes and try to be calm so we can figure this thing out." For what seemed like several minutes, Jimmy stroked my back. I coughed and sputtered, trying to expel something that felt like it was lodged in my throat. My mind knew nothing was actually stuck in there, but my lungs felt differently.

Jimmy's hands worked wonders, regulating my breathing and returning my strength. The numbness that had taken over my body began to fade away. I grasped the radio with both hands and attempted another radio call.

"Hamilton Field, please come in. This is Claret Lake Tower. Someone please answer me. Please. I'm begging you. Over." Static filled the radio waves again as I willed someone to hear me.

"Claret Lake Tower, this is Hamilton Army Air Field. Is this an Army Flash? Over."

"*Yes*, it's an Army Flash! We need help! A plane like I've never *ever* seen almost crashed into the tower! I can't find it on my charts anywhere. It's solid silver with no markings at all. And no propellers. *Not one.* I don't know if it's American or Japanese or...*German!*"

"Stand by Claret Lake Tower. Over."

"Lou, what was that thing?" Eddie screamed as he fell over the side of the tower, crashing onto the floor.

"I don't know, but I've got Hamilton Field on the radio. They said to stand by."

"That was by far the loudest sound I've heard in my life," Jimmy said. "That thing was huge and faster than anything I've ever seen. What kind of plane was it?"

"No idea. Can't find it on any of my sheets. See if you two can figure it out." I pulled papers from every drawer and threw them toward Eddie and Jimmy. "Maybe I missed something."

"Aunt Mary's trying to keep the other kids calm, but everyone's here." Jimmy said, pointing over the side of the tower. "It was all I could do to get them to stay on the ground and not come up here. They're scared. Really scared."

Static broke through the tension. "Claret Lake Tower, this is Hamilton Army Air Field. Are you still there?"

"Yes, the whole town is here."

"What exactly did you see? Over."

"I've never seen or heard anything like it. It sounded like a tornado and flew faster than any plane I've ever known. And it was flying *without* a propeller! It

73

was big and silver. It looked like a flying dolphin, or a whale. No markings, like I said before. Two wings, but *no propeller. How is that possible?* Over."

"Claret Lake Tower, what direction was it heading? Over."

"North-northeast at first. That's when it nearly crashed into the tower. When I finally picked myself up off the floor and realized I was still alive, I looked up and saw it banking toward the south. It flew so fast it's probably over Mexico by now. Or South America."

"Stand by Claret Lake Tower. Over."

"What do we do, Lou?" I heard Clay yell from the ground below. Leaning over the edge, I saw fear claiming every face. Silver whined as Becky clung to him, eyes as big as a harvest moon, her body shaking like a leaf in a windstorm.

"It's okay, everyone. Hamilton Field knows about it. We're just waiting to hear back from them."

"Claret Lake Tower, this is Hamilton Army Air Field. Come in. Over." I lunged for the radio and pressed the transmit button.

"This is Claret Lake Tower. Over."

"Good work, Claret Lake Tower. We have been in contact with the filter center controller at Muroc Field south of here. They are testing the range of a new type of aircraft. You've seen up close what not many people have. It's called a jet aircraft. It's an experimental fighter with jet-propelled engines. That's why you didn't see any propellers—it doesn't have any. The pilot thought he was in a non-populated area when he descended to just above treetop altitude to perform some tests and maneuvers. Please keep this sighting to yourself as it is a Top Secret project. Over."

"Roger, Hamilton Field. But we're out here in the middle of nowhere. Who on earth would I tell?"

CHAPTER 12

March, 1943

After many more meatless months, Ralph had still not mastered the art of hunting. He hadn't even minored in it. I had come to the conclusion he delighted in playing in the forest, picking blackberries and smearing them all over his face and arms, pretending to be an Indian in a western talkie. But so far, Ralph's hunting expeditions had been fruitless, except for the berries.

The yearning for fresh meat by the kids in town made me rethink my distaste for hunting. I had always been a good shot, ever since Papa bought me my first bolt-action .22 for my sixth birthday and taught me how to shoot. Back then, the only way I could pull the bolt out to charge it was to put the muzzle down in the dirt, lock my knees around it and pull up on the thing. I still do it that way.

I'd never shot anything, not a deer, not a pig, not even a squirrel. I accidentally hit a grey fluffy rabbit once, but I must have just grazed it because it hopped off into the woods after being frozen solid for a few seconds. At that moment, I felt like I'd been the one shot when I hit that poor, defenseless little rabbit. Shot me right through the heart.

"Come on," Jimmy said, drawing me back from the past and a reminiscent shiver. "Let's go get us a pig. I'm hungry for some bacon." He looked as happy as a kid on Christmas morning.

"Fine," I said, bucking up for what needed to be done. We walked north of town towards the forest bursting with bright green foliage and tiny blossoms, enjoying the first warm days of spring. Sauntering behind him, I noticed a round container filled his right back pocket.

"What's that in your pocket?" I asked him as naively as I could get away with, batting my eyes at him.

"Don't you give me any grief about my chewing tobacco," he said. "I'm practically a man now, so I can chew it if I want to." I knew he rarely chewed the stuff, but I liked to give him a hard time about it anyway.

A rabbit hopped out from behind an elderberry bush about twenty-five yards ahead. It saw us and froze in the middle of the path, not moving a muscle. My fears came roaring back as I halted in my steps, images flooding my memory of that rabbit all those years ago. I could practically hear it thinking, "If I just don't move, they won't see me."

Jimmy cocked his gun, and the rabbit's ears twitched as it turned its little dirty-white fluffy head toward us.

"I see you Mr. Rabbit," I called out, scaring the poor little beast back into the shadows of the elderberry bush, fully laden with tiny, tasty berries. "Mr. Rabbit sure knows a good bush when he sees it."

"Why'd you do that?" Jimmy stomped his foot, rolled his eyes and lowered his rifle. "I had the perfect shot."

"I thought we were here to hunt pigs, not rabbits," I said, winking at him as I brushed by him on the dirt path, sashaying past and listening to the dried leaves from last fall crunch underneath my boots with every step. "Let's keep going and spare Mr. Rabbit."

Jimmy shook his head and took the lead again. After our brief sparring, we settled down and tried to be quiet, which was easier in late summer when the leaves were still high above us and attached to the tree branches. We listened for rustling in the bushes, but it was almost two hours before we found what we were looking for.

A couple of blackberry bushes to the right of the path shook as if they were sprouting legs, ready to walk away. We stood on our tiptoes and spied two full-sized wild pigs snatching berries off the bush.

"They're so cute," I whispered, laying my head on Jimmy's shoulder, watching them rooting in the bushes like they'd found the Holy Grail.

"They're so tasty," Jimmy whispered back, licking his lips and raising his rifle to eye level, getting ready for the shot. "Circle around just over there to the right so you can grab 'em after I shoot. But stay back a bit so I don't shoot you."

"Thanks for thinking of me," I said flippantly and began tiptoeing through the brush. I tried to be as quiet as a field mouse. Finally crouching into position, I gave Jimmy a thumbs up.

Bang. The shot rang out through the forest, and the larger of the pigs squealed, well, like a pig. He ran into a tree standing beside him, then chose to bolt straight toward me, full speed ahead. How a pig could run like that after being shot was beyond me. The smaller pig ran in the complete opposite direction, ramming into the tree before jerking away from both of us and high tailing it toward the denser part of the forest.

Bracing myself for impact, I leapt up and landed squarely on top of the larger pig. Grabbing Mr. Pig's ears, I rode him like he was a bronc in the rodeo I saw with my parents down in 'Frisco years ago. But Mr. Pig proved to be much more slippery than a greased bronc, and he bolted out from under me and headed into the forest. Jimmy hadn't gotten a direct hit, but there was enough blood on my dungarees and hands to make me realize Mr. Pig wouldn't make it very far.

We tracked his blood trail until it ended in a pool. We saw the pig collapse beside a tall, moss-covered oak tree, panting and squealing, fighting to not give up the ghost just yet.

"Poor thing," I said, kneeling down into the dirt, stroking its pinkish ear that felt soft as silk. His wild, glazed eyes looked up at me, fear running rampant through them and yet begging for help at the same time. His breaths came out in deep rattles as the grunts and bellows became less and less powerful and more and more sad.

With a gentle touch, I stroked its soft head. "Thank you for giving your life so that we may have food, Mr. Pig."

The tribe taught me, above all, to respect the life of any animal you kill for food. I continued to do that, even if I wasn't the one doing the killing.

"I wonder if we can get Bev to fix us some good, crispy bacon tonight," Jimmy said, sauntering over with his rifle slung across his proud shoulder.

"Maybe so," I muttered, a sympathetic tear creeping down my cheek as Mr. Pig took his dying breath.

Jimmy unfolded a coarse burlap sack and tied a couple of ropes to the ends of it, constructing a makeshift stretcher large enough to drag the pig back to town. I slung my rifle over my shoulder and helped roll Mr. Pig onto the burlap for its last trip.

"This fella weighs a ton," I said, trying to pull on the ropes to no avail. Jimmy grabbed hold of one rope while I pulled the other. We didn't make very good time, but I saw McGregor's Hill in front of us. It led into town, and it was downhill all the way after that.

Anxious to reach the hill, I missed seeing a tree branch in the path half hidden by leaves and tripped right over it, losing my balance and landing with a thud in the middle of a coffeeberry shrub.

A sinister rattling sounded from underneath me. I immediately stiffened, like the rabbit in the path earlier.

Maybe if I don't move, it won't notice me. Not one muscle even dared to quiver.

"Don't move," Jimmy whispered. He gently placed his rope on the ground, cocked his rifle and moved slowly toward the bush. The rattlesnake shook its rattles again, its warning siren blaring directly underneath me, and I knew I was much too close to its lair.

"Jimmy, hurry," I whispered, my voice trembling in a sing-song cadence.

"Just sit tight."

"Easy for you to say," I whispered, my voice quivering with fear. I tried not to move, but fate was not happy with me that day, and I couldn't stifle the sneeze that wracked my body. The coffeeberry shrub collapsed underneath my weight, and I felt two fangs sharp as nails sink deep into my ankle.

"*Owww!*" I screamed, not caring if people in the next county heard me. "*Ow! Ow! Ow!* It got my ankle! Jimmy, *do something!*"

Jimmy sprinted forward and lifted me out of the bush as the olive-striped rattler slithered away, pleased with its defense of its territory.

"Don't move a muscle," he commanded, laying me in the middle of the path on a bed of leaves.

"I couldn't if I wanted to," I cried. "It hurts *bad.*"

"Hold still," Jimmy ordered. "You have that pocket knife your papa gave you?"

"In my right front pocket. *Hurry!*"

He held my swelling ankle in one hand and pulled out the knife with the other. "I know this is gonna hurt, so just go ahead and scream your head off."

He took my shoe off, threw it aside, rolled my holey wool sock away from the bite and proceeded to slice an "X" directly through the darkening bite.

A blood curdling scream crossed my lips. Jimmy winced at the sound.

"I may go deaf after that one," he said.

"I'm scared, Jimmy. Really scared. Papa got bit when I was little. Doc thought he might have to amputate Papa's foot. He almost *died.*"

"You're gonna be fine. I promise," Jimmy said, tossing the knife toward his rifle.

Passing out seemed to be my best option, but the adrenaline coursing through my veins wouldn't allow it. My asthma decided to strike, and I gulped for air like a guppy.

Jimmy used his hands and fingers to pump the blood out of the "X," trying to extract as much venom as he could before it congealed any of my blood. He switched between pumping my ankle with his hands and sucking the poisonous venom with his mouth, spitting the crimson red liquid into the pool of blood now covering the leaves.

The rhythmic feel of his hands on my ankle oddly had a calming effect, and after several minutes, the adrenaline rush began to subside as did my wheezing.

He took one hand away and reached into his back pocket quickly.

"Hold out your hand," he said. He flung a wad of chewing tobacco into my outstretched palm and then threw a clump into his mouth.

"Get to chewing, Lou," he said, pushing my hand toward my mouth.

"That's disgusting." I winced as pain shot through my ankle again and began to stream up my leg.

"Just do it."

The tobacco tasted smoky and tart. I tried not to swallow the juice, but a few drops made it past my tongue and dribbled down my throat. Coughs tormented my body as I spit the tobacco and what I could of the juice into Jimmy's hand which appeared quick as a wink under my drippy chin.

Jimmy spit his wad out on top of mine and let out a laugh. "You should see your face. Believe me, it's an acquired taste." He held his hand open and caught the leftovers I spit out. Placing the tobacco on the bite, he wrapped the sock around my ankle and cinched it tightly to keep the tobacco in place.

"If Mama were here, she'd probably put a tea bag on it," I said. Mama used tea bags for everything from sunburn to mosquito bites. My thoughts fell to past remedies, but the pain returned with a vengeance and brought me back to the present as quick as a rattlesnake can strike.

"I'm gonna have to carry you back to town to see Doc," he said. "Don't want that venom traveling through your system if we can help it, and walking would get it pumping something fierce."

"What about Mr. Pig?" I muttered.

"Clay and Murph can come back and get the pig. Ralph has been no help at all with hunting. Between you and me, I think he's afraid of the sight of blood." He picked me up out of the crimson-stained leaves and adjusted me in his arms.

"You okay, Pipsqueak?" he asked. "Try not to pass out. I need you awake."

I nodded, but my eyes couldn't focus. They fluttered shut, sleep threatening to take over after the adrenaline drained from my system.

"Mmm," I mumbled, shifting closer to his body and wrapping my arms around his neck. "I should get bit more often. This is nice."

The words barely left my lips before I drifted toward the dependable escape of sleep.

CHAPTER 13

"That should do it," Doc said, wrapping my ankle in a yellowed cloth bandage he dug out of an old army pack beside his mostly empty medicine cabinet. "Take it easy for the rest of today. And no climbing that tower for a couple of days. Have Eddie take over full time for you. If need be, have him bring little Becky to Aunt Mary's. She'll watch after her real good."

"I'll make sure she rests," Jimmy said as he sent me a wink. "It's my birthday, so she has to do what I say."

"Yeah, right," I answered, rolling my eyes his way and lingering on their soft brown color a little longer than usual. Lately I felt like I could disappear into them.

I shook my head and blinked a few times, trying to come out of the fog that had overtaken my senses. Jimmy slid his arms around my torso and underneath my legs and carried me out of Doc's office, wound and all.

As we exited Doc's, the midday sun shone so brightly I had to hold one hand over my eyes to shade my face. Silver trotted over, sniffed my bandage and whined. I reached down and gave him a quick pat on the head.

"I'm okay boy, just fine." I knew he felt guilty that he didn't join Jimmy and me on our hunting expedition, but he was so busy sleeping in the sun, I didn't want to disturb him.

"She's right as rain," Jimmy said to the crowd of children who had gathered after seeing him running into town with me unconscious in his arms. A round of applause erupted.

Little Becky tugged on his pant leg. "Miss Lou. She gonna be okay?" Becky tried to wipe away the trail of tears that streamed down her splotchy cheeks. Taken by her concern for me, I stretched out my hand and stroked the fine strands of her straggly brown hair that hadn't seen a pair of scissors for over a year.

"I'm just fine, Miss Becky," I reassured her. "You know there's not much that can keep this ole gal down. I'm just going to rest for a bit, then by tomorrow, you won't even know I got snake bit."

This seemed to reassure her, and after wiping a stray tear away, she skipped off hand in hand with Eddie. The pause that had been put on life turned into life as usual once again.

"Murph? Clay?" Jimmy turned his head toward my two friends. "Can you two go up to McGregor's Hill and haul back that pig? I really don't want any of those wild animals to grab it before we can get our bacon."

"Sure enough," Clay said. "You just take care of Lou and make sure she follows Doc's orders."

"Will do," Jimmy agreed, glancing at me to make sure I didn't make a fuss. How could I when I had discovered heaven in his arms?

"Let's go hang out by the lake," Jimmy said. He hauled me across town and turned to walk down the hill toward the dock behind my house, Silver trotting at his heels. My arms once again wrapped around his neck. It felt really good, really warm, just like home.

When we reached the dock, Jimmy walked to the end and gently knelt down, placing me on the worn wood and sat down beside me. He took off his shoes and socks and dangled his feet in the cool, clear water as Silver laid his head in my lap. It began warming up a bit earlier in the week, and the water beckoned us to play. A fish jumped up beside Jimmy's toes as he wiggled them, playing with the curious lake resident.

We sat in companionable silence until the sun began to disappear behind Mount Callisto. Jimmy remained completely silent until he took a deep breath, letting it out in one long whoosh. He stared at the mountain in the distance, but his eyes seemed a million miles away.

"Lou, I got my letter."

I had completely forgotten that not only was it his birthday, but it was his eighteenth birthday.

"When?" I asked.

"Within the week." He pulled one foot out of the water and raised his knee to his chest, resting his chin atop it as the water trickled down his leg and pooled around us.

"Oh Jimmy," I cried out, reaching my arms around him and holding him with all my might. Maybe if I gripped him tightly enough, he couldn't go away. "This is the day I've been dreading. I hate the thought of you going off to war. It scares me, Jimmy."

Another of my dependable rocks was being pulled out from underneath me. I felt the war already taking him away, surrounding me with loneliness settling in for the long haul. And he hadn't even left yet.

"Honestly, it scares the tarnation out of me too, Lou," he said, rubbing my back gently and resting his chin on the top of my head. "But I don't have a choice."

Tears started to make a beeline down my cheeks for the second time today. I tried to stop them, but the realization hurt even more than the snake bite. He cradled my face in his warm, rough hands and looked deep into my tear-filled eyes.

"I'll do everything I can to be safe. I promise." And then he kissed me for the first time.

CHAPTER 14

Emptiness enveloped the valley the day after Jimmy left. I didn't want to be in the tower alone, so I enlarged the pack I carried on my back in order to hoist Silver up with me. When we got to the top, Silver's sixth sense kicked into high gear, and he consoled me the way only a loyal dog can—curling up beside me, laying his chin on my foot, and letting out a slight whimper to let me know he cared.

One benefit of having tower watch duty was that you could have a good cry and no one saw you. Since Jimmy left, all I wanted to do was cry, so I curled up in the corner of the tower with Silver in my arms and gave in to the pain. By the end of my watch, I wouldn't have a dry thread on the front of my shirt, and Silver wouldn't have any dry fur on his body.

After what felt like a few hours but was probably only about fifteen minutes, I pulled myself together, stood and moved to the desk to grab the field glasses. *Time to study the sky*, I thought. *Maybe it'll get my mind off Jimmy.*

Ever since I started tower duty, I'd only seen a few American military planes and the jet aircraft. I figured the gasoline rations spread nationwide, so no one was able to fly the little Beech's and tandems just for the fun of it. The Coast Guard rode on horseback along the shoreline to spot any enemy activity in the waters bordering our country, but the spotting towers went as far inland as eighty to a hundred miles and dotted the landscape every twenty miles up and down the California coast.

My tower sat about seventy miles east of the Pacific as the crow flies. I used the old pair of field glasses that came with the tower to scan the skies and continued to study the sheets describing what aircraft to look for. Other areas outside Lagune County used adults as spotters, but then the government hadn't filed an incorrect census report for them.

During my tower watch, I looked for forest fires, too. I figured I might as well. It passed the time. While I was on duty, I liked to pin on the Volunteer Aircraft Observer patch the government sent in the box with the instructions. It had a three-bladed white propeller embroidered atop a cobalt blue circle just three inches across. Underneath was the top edge of an inverted red triangle. When I left, I placed the sturdy fabric patch under the radio so it wouldn't blow away.

"I wish Jimmy were here," I sighed, looking at the patch and then down at Silver who delivered a consoling whimper.

"It's okay, boy," I said, patting his head. "I'm just missing him, that's all."

Content that he had taken care of me for the moment and successfully completed his canine duty, he curled up by my feet but continued to watch me closely.

To get my mind off of Jimmy, I studied the banner the government sent again and tested myself by teaching Silver about the different plane silhouettes.

"Come over here, boy," I said, patting the side of my trouser legs. "See, this one is an American plane. You can tell by the flatter wingtips, the larger fuselage and the squared-off shape of its tail. And this one has an inverted gull wing. Also, our planes have what they call 'in-line' engines—they are more streamlined. The Japanese ones have big 'radial' engines—much rounder and bulkier."

He wagged his tail and placed his paw on the planes.

"Good boy," I said, continuing with the lesson.

"Now, here's a tricky one. Is this Japanese or American?"

Silver got quiet, as if he wanted to make sure to answer correctly.

"I know what you're thinking," I said. "It's a trick question. But it's not. When in doubt, if there's a big red dot on it, it's always Japanese."

A bark filled the air.

"Very good. You pass the test."

Silver settled down to take a nap as I grabbed the field glasses, buffed off the lenses, adjusted the magnification, and observed the sky around the mountains surrounding Claret Lake. I knew the Japanese planes by heart. If a German one were to fly by, I might have had a problem. The towers on the east coast had banners depicting those planes, but out on the west coast, the government just wanted us to know the Japanese ones.

"Japan is a long way away, Silver, but their ships can get close enough that their planes could possibly reach us here at Claret Lake."

We stayed in the tower for an extra four hours simply because I didn't want to face the rest of the town's knowing eyes yet. Jimmy's departure weighed heavily on my mind, and I knew the tears would well up again in an instant.

I surveyed the dusky sky draping the valley in colors of orange, yellow and blood red. Scanning the tree line, my field glasses focused on Rex staring my way. Even though he stood a good two hundred yards north of the tower, I had no doubt he could see me. I lifted a hand to wave, and he nodded his head before turning toward the forest, disappearing from sight. He knew how much I missed Jimmy.

That night, I imagined Jimmy watching the sun slip past the horizon with me from wherever he was. It felt oddly embarrassing, but I actually missed Jimmy more than Mama and Papa. Maybe it's because he was the last one to go, or maybe it's because he was the one person I depended on after Mama and Papa left.

CHAPTER 15

September, 1943

Summer faded to fall as we continued to survive. September and October were always busy in our part of northern California with the walnut, pear and grape harvests coming in. The fruity scents filled the air, beckoning us toward the slopes and their juicy, sweet offspring. One whiff of the aromatic breeze crossing the lake proved the pears and grapes were ripe for the picking.

Bev brought us breakfast plates of canned beans and Julie's fresh bread. It seemed we were eating a lot of beans and bread lately. I made a mental note to check the food reserves.

"I saw the walnuts yesterday when I was out riding," Barbara said at breakfast, the third sunny day of September. "There aren't a lot, but Bev and Julie should be able to get a few meals out of them."

"Thanks," I said, turning to ask Murph and Tommy what had happened to the crop this year. They huddled together, muttering quietly, trying to ignore me.

Julie emerged from the general store with a stack of leftover burlap sacks for collecting the walnuts.

"Murph? Tommy? Is there anything I should know about?" I asked, sitting down in the squeaky chair next to them.

"Um, Lou? We didn't do so good with the walnuts and the pears. The grapes turned out better, but not great. We just don't know what happened. I think they did better when Jimmy was around." They bowed their heads, trying not to look me in the eye.

I swallowed the pain that always welled up when someone mentioned Jimmy's name.

"Well, let's go take a look and see what we've got," I said, rising from the chair and grabbing a bag from Julie who handed them out to everyone.

We walked as a group around the lake to the slopes of Mount Callisto where the walnuts grew. Murph and Tommy shuffled slowly toward the back of the crowd. Clay stayed behind to row Papa's boat over so we didn't have to lug the walnut haul back by foot. They weren't too heavy after they were shelled, but those shells could be mighty weighty.

As we approached the walnut fields, everyone saw the pitiful showing for the year.

"What in the world happened here?" Clay asked, stepping ashore and grounding the boat behind us. Every eye on the mountain focused on Tommy and Murph.

"We did the best we could, but they just wouldn't grow," Murph whispered, pretending to be preoccupied with drawing a masterpiece in the black sand at his feet with his toe.

"It's okay," I said, walking over and giving him a pat on the back which proved to be a feat, given how much he had grown over the summer. "It's been a bad year for a lot of things. Even the tribe has had trouble finding food."

We trudged through the black soil and plucked what was left of the walnuts from the branches of the trees. Their brown shells had multitudes of black spots on them, and a good amount were broken open, their meat littering the gritty soil. Occasionally, one or two of the diamonds made it into a pocket or a sack along with the walnuts that grew amongst them on Mount Callisto's giving slopes. Because of where they grew, we had called them "diamond walnuts" for years.

The boat remained half-empty after all the bags of walnuts were brought aboard. Since extra room abounded, I joined Clay for the row back over.

After we were out of earshot of the others, he let out a groan.

"This does not look good," he said.

"I know, Clay." I grimaced at the pitiful number of sacks. "I'm afraid Julie and Bev won't have much to bake with this year. Did you see the pear trees and grapes? They're practically just as bad as the walnuts. We're going to have a problem come winter. I saw Rex yesterday, and he told me the tribe is having trouble finding food, too. We'll share this with him and have the girls do what they can with the rest."

Clay nodded in agreement and continued rowing toward disaster.

Julie baked the best of the walnuts into pies and breads. We enjoyed a succulent treat and all ate much more than we expected, but the walnuts were in their prime and the survivors tasted so good. Their woodsy flavor and aroma mixed with the husky scent of molasses filled the empty stomachs and souls around the restaurant's lean tables, and we all slept through the night with full bellies.

Morning came early as it does during the harvest season, and we all hiked back to Mount Callisto to pick the pears after a less than cheerful breakfast of the last of the fresh walnut bread.

Row after row of pear trees typically sagged from the weight of the fruit. At least they did in the past. But the trees were on strike and didn't yield us a very large crop.

"We'll be lucky to get a few pies out of these," Julie said, shaking her curls vigorously. "And I don't think many are fit for preserving."

We picked them, nonetheless, and gobbled up pears and pear pies for dinner. Julie said a prayer and spread the last of the sugar over the remaining pears, staying behind the next morning to start the canning process.

For the rest of us, the next day was grape harvesting day. The grapes usually came in at the same time as the pears, but since it was a little more difficult to harvest them, it took all the rest of us.

"You haven't lived until you've harvested grapes," Murph said, kneeling among the vines and eating more juice-filled fruits than he collected. A sugary aroma settled over the fields, sweet, tart, and grapey. The vineyard had been in his family for generations. He was a pro at everything grape and was just glad to be out reaping the reward from his crop-tending.

"At least he did a better job with the grapes," Clay muttered beside me in the soil. "The pears and walnuts? Now that's another story."

"Look here," Murph said, grabbing the cutting tool from me. The harvesting tool looked like a box cutter with a hook. "You're doing it all wrong. You hold onto the grape stem like this and cut this way. Take your time. Baby them."

Grabbing the knife back from him, I started slashing at the unruly, tough vines my way. After about the fifth one, I stared down to see my hands were the same color as the grapes, lingered a bit too long and all of a sudden realized my finger really hurt.

"You did it, didn't you," he chuckled. "You missed the stem and sliced right through your finger. I told you this was tough work and you have to take your time and baby the vines. But would you listen to me? No."

"No grape stomping for you today," Clay said, loading me into the boat to row me back to town for a few stitches and a meal of crow.

After a quick trip to see Doc, I was all bandaged up and ready to attack those grapes again. But when we got back to the field, a heavenly fruity aroma filled the air, and we saw everyone dancing around in barrels lined with grapes, stomping the succulent purple fruits with their bare feet.

"They're squishy and cold, Miss Lou," Becky squealed.

"Every one of you is as purple as those grapes," I said, laughing at the sight but inside, grateful they were able to have a little glimpse of fun. "Just remember, there's no giggle water to be made. Prohibition may be over, but we need the grapes for food. Just make sure we have enough for canning. Or for dinner for that matter."

"Let's hope so," Clay said, popping a plump purple grape into my mouth.

CHAPTER 16

"Lou, are you listening? Your report, please." Aunt Mary tapped her nub of a pencil on the pitted schoolhouse desk. Not many of us had been vigilant about going to school, so we voted to only have class one day a week come autumn. Every Monday we either read a report we had written or recited multiplication tables, depending on the age of who was presenting. Today was my day to read my report, but my mind wandered to more important things, like the war raging overseas and wondering if Jimmy was doing okay in the Pacific.

"Yes ma'am," I said as I rose from my chair and strode up to the front of the class to deliver my report.

The floorboards squeaked with every step I took. Someone built the old schoolhouse in 1859. Windows graced only one side of it, and a potbellied stove and a few other ancient props from the late-nineteenth century populated the inside. During peacetime, two teachers taught at the school for all twelve grades, and they typically were not spring chickens. It appeared that during wartime, Aunt Mary always took over. The schoolhouse was far from adequate, and on top of the lack of teachers, the building was a firetrap. No way could it withstand a Japanese invasion.

I stood in front of the chalkboard, cleared my throat and began. "When I Became a Japanese—I mean, an Indian."

Clay and Murph chuckled at my mistake.

"As you all know, there's an island behind my house. It's a peninsula, actually, but when the water rises, it looks like an island. Technically and legally, it belongs to us, but it has a lot of Indian things on it since they've hunted there for generations. I've found arrowheads, spearheads, grinding stones, slings and several stone pillars. My mama and papa are friends with the Indian chief, Rex, and many of the people in his tribe, and they let them use the land to hunt. Because of this, the tribe lets Papa hunt with them."

Fiddlesticks. I forgot to put in the most important part. I put the report down, looked out at the class, and started to improvise.

"You see, the island is sacred to the Indians, so they took us into their tribe so that someone from the tribe would own the island. They used to use the island for some of their tribal ceremonies and for hunting. As you all know, they are the tribe with the tule boats. Tules are reeds. Their boats are like the Egyptian boats with bundles of fibers all strung together. Like the one they put Moses in—in the Bible. Tule reeds are really thick like cattail weeds, but much thicker and very buoyant. They trap air, and as long as you don't break the outside skin on them, they'll float a pretty hefty load. But if you break them, they're like a sponge. Anyways..."

Where was I? Lifting my report back up, I quickly found my place.

"Because the Indians feel the island is sacred, they believe the owner of the land should be a tribal member, so they had Mama and Papa and me become "blood" members of their tribe. When I was four years old, we went to one of their pow-wows. It was held at night. They formed a large circle in the dirt with earth banked up around it. They covered the circle with a canvas tent that had an open flap on one side. They said it was a little different from their usual smoke house, but there was a hole in the center of the tent that let the smoke from the fire out. The women and children sat around the back edge of the circle, and the men sat near the center. In the very center was a dancing ring that they had buried washtubs underneath. In the old days, they used to bury drums, but they don't do that anymore. Some of the men were musicians who played fluted sticks while the chanting went on. In the middle were two dancers. One of them was Rex's son who was grown. The only things he wore were a loin cloth and a blind fold. A live snake had been sewn into the blindfold so it moved all the time."

I tried not to emphasize the word 'snake' because little Becky might squeal, which she did right on queue. Snakes terrified Becky after that rattler bit me. On the other hand, the boys all whooped and clapped.

"Swell!" Murph said, leaning forward in his seat and smiling.

Time to get back on track.

"Rex's son held two snakes—one in each hand, but I asked Papa and he said they weren't rattlesnakes."

Becky breathed a sigh of relief and relaxed in her desk chair.

"The medicine man was the second dancer. He wore a little bit more than Rex's son because he also had on a leather shirt, but he had a dreadful time getting into the tent because his headdress was so big. It was a huge white cap that covered his entire head except for his eyes and nose. Tall sticks with red, white and black feather balls on the ends poked out from all around the cap. The sticks were what got caught in the tent flap. Other members of the tribe helped him, and he finally made it inside. The two dancers danced in the center of the tent around the fire that burned in the middle. Since they were dancing on top of the buried tubs, it sounded like they were drumming and chanting at the same time. They pricked my wrist until it bled. Each of the Indians did the same to their wrists, and they rubbed our blood together and we were blood brothers."

"Did that hurt?" Becky asked.

"Not that I remember. I know I didn't cry."

"When times got tough during the depression, the government would only let us hunt during certain times, so during the times we weren't allowed to hunt, the tribe let us camp on their reservation and do our hunting with them. So while Mama and Papa went out hunting, I played with some of the kids from the tribe. The government said the Indians could hunt anytime the wanted, so since Papa let them hunt on the island, they would come here to hunt ducks and geese when it got cold in the winter and food was scarce. And they shared their deer and rabbit meat with us. Many people went hungry during those days, but they made sure we had plenty to eat. We were members of their tribe. And that's how I became an Indian," I said and made my way back to my desk.

"Very good, Lou," Aunt Mary said. "And we all appreciate everything you and your family have shared with us during the rough winter months. It helps us out during the tough times."

With the shortage of meat even for the tribe, it looked like more tough times were just around the corner.

CHAPTER 17

October, 1943

When I was about a year old, Mama said she discovered I would crawl down to the lake and just be looking at the rocks. I would get down on my hands and knees and put my face down straight in the water. She knew I was going to drown, so she had Aunt Mary keep an eye on me. But I was never afraid of the water and kept doing it.

As a kid growing up, I used to like to go out and sit on the wall by the lake behind our house and just look. Look and listen. The good Lord made nature beautiful, and I just enjoyed it. I watched the birds with their skilled wings in flight. Listened to the coarse call of the cranes. Watched the spooked coots slap the water with their lobed toes to get away from the mallards and red-billed mergansers that itched to play with them. I imagined where I would fly off to if I could.

More than ever, I wanted to fly away and explore more of the world.

It had been seven months since Jimmy left. The summer of my sixteenth year crept in quietly on the heels of spring. Its hot, humid days faded into fall and arrived with autumn's cool, breezy days. But the days had a dark cast over them with everything that had gone on. How were the kids in town supposed to keep their spirits up while I wallowed in my worry over the war and fretted over the lack of food? Looking out over the water, I longed for the days when I didn't have a care in the world, complained about swimming across the lake, and could just watch nature around me, taking for granted that I would have a meal to come home to and open arms to hug me when I walked into my house.

With the scent of straw wafting up from south of the lake, I realized haying season had arrived. Walking back up the dock, I put my hands around my lips and called out.

"Haying season. Let's go everybody. Time to get to work."

Bowerton, a tiny town just south of Claret Lake, had the largest hay ranch in the area with the most hay to be harvested. Silver, the boys and I marched through the woods. We reached a clearing, pushed back the tree branches, and saw the fields of yellow hay swaying in the autumn breeze, rippling like the sea, wave after wave.

Ole man Granger's tractor sat near an old wooden barn to the west, and we all watched as Clay attached the reaper to it, which cut the hay. He swung up onto the rusty red contraption and fiddled with the switches. Finally, the ancient piece of farm equipment coughed and sputtered to life. Clay straightened his shoulders and looked very proud of himself.

"You only have whatever gas is in the tractor, and that's it," I yelled. "Make sure to get the heaviest areas first. After you cut the hay, Murph and the boys here will roll and tie it into bales."

Clay raised his right hand and started to speak.

"And yes, Bev packed sandwiches for you when you're done." I said this before he could get a word in edgewise.

He smiled and nodded his head, his unruly hair swaying back and forth.

"Thanks, Lou," he grinned. "You can read my mind."

The tractor chugged into the field as Silver, awaiting my nod of approval, chased after the mechanical beast, barking up a blue streak.

I chuckled as I turned back toward the basket Bev and Julie packed for us to double check and make sure I hadn't told a falsehood. Pulling the red and white checked cloth back, I saw the makings of a small meal. Our food supplies were running low, but at least we had a few pieces of bacon left.

I leaned back against an old hickory tree and took in the scene: boys toiling in the field, doing the work of grown men; a basket full of food prepared by girls doing the work of grown women; and a hungry girl nibbling on a piece of stale hay in the middle of the town she's trying to save.

Glancing toward the cloud of smoke in the distance that followed the tractor like a young eager puppy, I caught sight of a horse silhouetted against the distant sky. I didn't start riding horses until I was about eight or nine. Barbara's father had that old buckskin even back then, and we'd ride double, sometimes with a saddle, sometimes without.

"That crazy buckskin will outlive all of us," I said. I gave a shrill whistle, and she sauntered across the pasture, hoping a carrot awaited her in my hand. The old girl deserved a treat, too, so I dug into Bev's basket and came up with a container of canned carrots. Straining, I popped open the jar and poured the darkened orange disks into my hand, the syrup slipping through my fingers and plopping onto the dry ground.

Bucky whinnied her approach, lowered her head and sniffed at the treats in my hand.

"Go ahead, girl," I said. "Barbara and Fern work post office duty today, so it's just you and me." I held out my hand covered in slimy sliced carrots and offered her the bounty. "I know canned isn't near as good as fresh, but it's nice to have something other than hay every once in a while."

Her fuzzy muzzle tickled my hand as she blew out a warm breath and took a few pieces, shaking her blonde mane that shimmered in the morning sunlight.

"Good, huh," I said. She lapped up the rest that I placed in my hand, and then sniffed around for more.

"That's all she wrote," I said, wiping my hands on top of the dust covering my dungarees and then gave her neck a good rub.

Oddly, she reached her long neck down past me and rubbed her muzzle against the back of my right knee, then bit at my left one.

"*Ouch! That hurts!*" I screamed, grabbing my knees, trying to rub away the pain. I never knew her to be forceful with Barbara or Fern, but she kept nudging at my knees.

"Stop that! *Bad horse!*" It took all my strength to get her to move her long muscular neck, but I finally won. She gave a quick neigh, trotted toward a shade tree, and went back to nibbling on hay.

I rubbed the back of my knees and realized that they really, really hurt. I couldn't believe she bit me. Twice. A fiery heat leapt inside my muscles, growing into a flaming burn I couldn't put out no matter how hard I rubbed it.

Looking up I saw Clay chugging toward me on the tractor. The boys were done with their first round of rolling and tying hay bales and followed the tractor to where the vittles resided.

"What's wrong?" Clay asked, turning off the motor and sliding down from the driver's seat.

"I'm not sure, but I think Bucky bit me. My knees are killing me. They've been hurting for a while, but nothing like this."

"Let me take a look," Clay said. "Stand up for a sec."

I struggled to stand up, but leaning on his shoulder, I finally straightened enough for him to roll up my trouser legs.

"*Holy mackerel,*" he screamed, and then let out a whistle.

"Stop, Clay. That's not funny."

"I was whistling at that." He pointed to the back of my knees. I twisted and turned, trying to see what he meant.

"I can't see it from here. What is it?"

"I have no idea," he said, shaking his head. "But I think Doc needs to take a look at it."

CHAPTER 18

Come winter, I simply couldn't take the pain anymore. I broke down and hobbled into Doc's office, Clay on my heels.

"You again," Doc said. "You just can't seem to stay out of harm's way. Give me just a minute." He turned back toward the town's littlest patient.

"Now Miss Becky, be sure to stick this copper penny in your mouth and get it all covered in spit and stick it on your wart. Do this every day, three times a day for the next week, and that mean old wart will be long gone in no time."

"No foolin'?" she questioned, turning the penny over in the palm of her little hand, tracing the ridges of it with her second finger.

"No foolin'," he answered, patting her on the head.

"Okay, Doc. I'll do that if you say I have to," Becky said, walking by us looking more pleased to have her very own copper penny than to be getting rid of her pesky wart.

"Come on in," Doc said, motioning us into his barren examining room.

Clay chose to stay in the waiting area while I walked toward the examining table and climbed up, the pain in my knees screaming with every movement.

Glancing toward Doc's desk, I saw a bottle of his favorite whiskey sitting on it, front and center, next to a pile of letters. I sent up a quick prayer that he hadn't started drinking yet today.

"It's my knees, Doc," I said, wincing at the pain from crawling up on the table. "They haven't gotten any better."

"Roll up those trouser legs, Lou, so I can take a peek at them."

I rolled the worn fabric up over my boney knees and turned on my side.

"Hmm," he muttered, applying pressure to the back of my knees that made me squeal like Mr. Pig when Jimmy shot him. "Can't say as I've seen this type of infection 'round here before, but I saw similar things in the war. We're gonna have to get this out of you. Could be gangrene."

"Are you serious?" I shrieked, rising up from the table ready to leap off and run to the next county.

"Um, is there anything I can do?" Clay asked, tentatively sticking his head around the door into the examining room.

"Lay back down, Lou," Doc said. "And stay still. I need to think." He walked to the bookshelf next to his desk and ran his finger over the dusty titles as he searched for help. A cracked red leather bound edition with gold leafing around the edges caught his eye. He pulled it out and searched for an answer, thumbing through the aged, yellowed pages as gold flecks drifted to the floor.

"Whatcha lookin' for?" Clay asked.

Doc held up an old, gnarled finger and shushed him. He sat down at his desk and pulled some papers from the top drawer. Clay and I looked at each other, shrugged our shoulders, and looked back toward Doc who thumped a page in the book with one finger and a letter on his desk with another.

"Well girlie, this isn't going to be easy," he said, glancing back at me.

I gathered my knees toward my chest, pain and all, and held them tight.

"What exactly do you mean by not easy?" Clay questioned.

My stomach began a preemptive churning of uneasiness as the acid started gurgling and flowing.

"If this is indeed related to gangrene," Doc said, "this infection absolutely has to be taken care of. And the only way to do that is surgery. I have to dig it out until it's all gone."

"Okay," I said. "So get me some knock-out medicine and let's get going." I knew that I had no choice if I wanted to get rid of the infernal flames burning inside my knees that made me feel like Julie could bake a cake on the heat emanating from them.

"That's the problem, girlie," he said, scratching the gray whiskers lining his chin. "We're plum out of knock-out medicine. The war's taken all we have, and this letter here says there's no more to be had 'til the war's over. It's all needed for the wounded soldiers."

"So can we just wait until after the war? I'm sure it's not that bad." My heart plunged toward my toes and took my breath and my crackly voice with it.

"Sorry girlie, that's not an option." He placed his hands on the table on either side of me and looked me squarely in the eye. "And I've got more bad news. You've got it behind both knees. If we don't get it out, it could work its way into your bones and infect them. Then you'd be up the creek without a paddle. Your folks would tan my hide if I didn't do right by you and take it out now."

"I'll be right here with you, Lou," Clay said, reaching for my hand and swallowing his fear.

"Thanks," I muttered, scared out of my wits, stuck with yet another hopeless situation.

We watched Doc strike a match and disinfect a slew of sharp metal tools with the flame. Clay started sweating like a horse after a full gallop around the lake, but all I felt was cold seeping into my core, knowing that if I survived this, I could survive anything.

Doc grabbed the bottle of whiskey and poured a shot.

"You're not going to start drinking now are you?" I said incredulously. "How can you drink now, of all times?!"

But instead of drinking it, he walked over and handed me the shot of whiskey.

"Nope, girlie. This is for you. Drink it up," he said, then he handed me the bottle.

The moment the metal instrument sliced into my flesh, a scream ripped through the room like there was no tomorrow. Pain seared through my skin and cut deep into my soul. I heard someone screaming like a banshee, and looking in the mirror on the wall, I realized the scream came from me. I saw Clay reflected in the mirror just before he crumpled into a heap by the door, passed out like a drunkard.

Doc handed me a pillow.

"Chew it up, honey," he said.

And I did, and he kept digging into my knees.

CHAPTER 19

February 1944

"Anyone who tells me I don't know what pain is is a big fat liar," I said to Silver as we sat on the dock, my favorite place to recuperate after my follow-up visits to Doc's. "Doc says it's good I've been sleeping in a chair with nothing under my legs and propping my feet up with a blanket lying on top to keep me warm."

It had been a cold winter that I couldn't have survived without Eddie. He tended the fire to keep me warm since I couldn't wear dungarees or anything that would touch my knees, only the skirts Mama would have been so proud to see me wear.

"I can't believe I don't have any scars. Doc did a good job." I rubbed Silver's silky smooth fur, enjoying the warmth he gave. "You know, it's interesting. We've been through a lot since Mama and Papa went away. We've done a lot of growing. A lot of learning. We've been through a lot of pain. Well, I have anyway," I said, rubbing the back of my knees.

Silver licked my hand. It seemed he understood full well what I meant. I was still tender behind the knees, but they were mostly healed.

"Thinking back on it, Bucky was just warning me about my knees. Horses have a sixth sense about them, kind of like you do. As much as I don't like horses, I've got to hand it to her. She probably saved my life."

Occasionally I stopped by to carry Bucky some carrots, but as of that day, we were officially out of food.

I stared at the lake through the kitchen window where Mama used to stand to watch Papa and me return from my mandatory morning swim. I complained so often about having to do it when my toes felt like they would freeze. What I wouldn't give now to have Papa in the boat beside me, rowing across the lake, waiting for me to collect my prize diamond. I actually missed those cold morning swims.

I hadn't swum to Mount Callisto since he left for the war. Since everybody left.

It had been two years and three months to the day since the emissaries visited Claret Lake. So much had changed by the twilight of my sixteenth year.

The kids just weren't old enough to keep running a town. They needed their parents. Frustration seemed to be overtaking everybody. Murph and Tommy couldn't get the fields to produce at all. Bev and Julie didn't know how to plan meals well, and the food had either been eaten in excess or gone bad since all the ice in the icebox finally melted. Ralph may have loved the outdoors, but he was no hunter. Clay couldn't get a single fish to bite anymore. And no one, absolutely no one, listened in school. I didn't know why we even bothered to have class anymore.

A heavy snow fell from the dark heavens, blanketing the valley and covering any evidence of movement from the day before. I couldn't remember the last time the dark gray clouds parted to let sunbeams through to warm the valley. It seemed Claret Lake had been shrouded in low hanging clouds—and matching moods—for months.

My feet had grown as had the rest of me, so pulling on my snow boots proved to be quite a challenge. They were almost too small to get on. I knew I might have to graduate to Papa's before long. I grabbed my favorite wool coat that had picked up a few rips and tears along the way and seemed to have shrunk in the process. I took some newspaper from the kindling bin on the edge of the hearth, a threadbare pair of mittens, and headed outside with Silver.

We started our trek toward the island. My island. My refuge. My place to think. My place to scream. The water was not quite low enough for the peninsula to be exposed, so we forded the short passageway and made our way to our private world. Mount Callisto stood sentinel in the distance, still shrouded by the darkness that enveloped the valley and wouldn't let go.

I needed to think. To plan. To figure out how to get us out of this mess. About the only thing left working that week was the pump house, and it decided to quit that morning.

Silver led the way across the island to the shore facing west, and I spread some newspaper over the ground and sat down. I glanced at the mountain, so strong, so ever-present, so dependable.

How could things have gone so wrong?

Silver snuggled close to console me as I buried my face in his soft, comforting fur.

"What are we going to do, boy?" I asked.

"You survive, Little One," a deep voice answered.

I turned around, startled to see Rex standing there. Silver perked up his ears and thumped his tail on the ground.

Rex's shadow loomed over me. One hand held a lone dead rabbit and the other draped a warm, thick blanket across my cold shoulders. The dense woven fabric coupled with deer hide kept the winter's chill at bay and was a welcome barrier to the morning frost.

He joined me on the snowy ground beside Silver as I unfolded more newspaper and spread it out to share with him. He nodded his thanks, looked downward and hesitated, shaking the snow from his feet, then settled in beside me.

"Why do you cry, Little One?" he asked, crossing his legs and placing his hands on his knees, staring out across the lake.

"I don't know what to do." My shoulders shook, not from the cold, but from the frustration of being a complete failure. I lowered my head to my callused hands, and the pent up frustration from years of challenges and shortcomings overtook me.

"Mama and Papa left me in charge of the town, in charge of everything, and it has been one disaster after another. I've tried everything I know to make it work. But now we have no food and no supplies. The kids are hungry, and I have no food for them. What am I supposed to do?"

"Hmm," he murmured, nodding his head slowly up and down.

We sat together, silent, listening to the crickets singing and the grasshoppers munching on dried up leaves. The early morning sounds of the lake somehow survived the cold, piercing winds of winter.

I laid my head on his shoulder, an accomplishment I couldn't have made a year ago when I was shorter.

"Do you remember the legend of the moon tears, Little One?" His deep voice startled me once again, breaking the silence just before dawn.

I searched my memories for the ancient legend. "It began a long time ago when a chieftain and the moon fell deeply in love. They danced. They celebrated. They loved. But the moon had responsibilities. She lit the nighttime for people around the world and also changed the seasons. As much as the moon wanted to stay, she knew she had to leave her love to fly through the sky. Clear, loving tears filled her eyes. She wept as she left her one true love. She wept many moon tears."

"Look at the mountain, Little One," Rex said. "See the moon tears? They shimmer in the light of the new day. The moon had to leave her love, but she left him many priceless gifts, many moon tears to remember her by."

I glanced westward toward Mount Callisto. The morning fog lifted, and sunbeams leapt over our shoulders to dance with the gems on her slopes.

"Remember the legend, Little One. And the moon's flight. They will help save you."

We sat in silence again, side by side. The chief and the little one. I tried to figure out what he meant, but as usual, if he spoke more than one word, he spoke in riddles, and my brain was tired.

"Remember, you can fly like the moon, Little One," he said. "You need nourishment to complete your task." He placed the body of the dead rabbit behind me in the snow.

"Thank you," I said, reaching out to squeeze his warm hand.

We continued to sit in companionable silence as Silver yawned and stretched his legs in his slumber. Rex studied the newspaper on the ground, running his calloused, dark fingers over the printed words for what seemed like forever but was probably the length of several deep breaths.

He rose, folded the newspaper slowly, meticulously, as if it was worth a year's trapping of food in the wilderness or another kind of fortune, and placed it carefully in my lap. He patted it with his hand a couple of times and turned to leave.

"Thank you, Rex, for the blanket, the food and the company. You can calm me when no one else can. I don't think I could have gone on without you here this morning." A genuine smile spread across my face as he turned to speak once more.

"Be aware of what you have, Little One. Observe. Remember the past. It leads to the future." He turned and walked north of town. I sat once more and stared toward the mountain.

Memories flooded my consciousness. The morning swims. The diamonds. The emissaries. The war. The tears. The survival. The desperation. The moon tears.

I glanced down at the newspaper still clutched in my hand. I scanned a grainy photograph from the war, straining to find Papa among the men, but he wasn't there. Under the picture, a single word caught my eye: *diamonds*.

I held the paper higher, out of the shadows, and read:

DIAMONDS NEEDED

J.G. Brothers Manufacturing, San Francisco, California

Diamonds may be every woman's dream, but during wartime, they are every shipbuilder's dream, every engineer's dream, every manufacturer's dream. As our society shifts toward building ships and other tools necessary to defend our country, we are experiencing a shortage of diamonds in our business. We need diamonds to embed in our cutting wheels, for sanding and etching, and most importantly, for mechanisms and for polishing ball bearings. If you or anyone you know has access to diamonds they are willing to part with for the war effort, please phone us at DO uglas 0519 or come by our plant on Pier Eight, the Embarcadero, San Francisco.

I placed the paper back in my lap and focused on the slopes that seemed to be calling to me from across the lake. The diamonds danced in the morning sunbeams like never before, and suddenly everything was clear—as clear as the moon's tears.

Silver followed me as I ran across the island, waded through the water, jumped up onto the dock, and raced past the plane that had not moved since the emissaries emerged from it over two years ago. I took the winterizing tarp off the rowboat that had not seen use since Clay used it to haul the walnuts. After wiping a colony of spider webs off the wooden plank stretched across the craft, I whistled for Silver to get in. He jumped into a couple of inches of water in the bottom of the boat and shook as I grabbed the oars and climbed in. I scooped out a few handfuls of water and began the trek across the lake.

"Rowing such a distance is tiring for a Little One who has not exercised in a very long time," I said, panting along with Silver. "I must start swimming again soon. What do you think?"

Silver licked my hand with his rough, wet tongue.

I rowed as more and more energy filled my tired limbs the closer we got to Mount Callisto. The breeze off the lake filled my nostrils and fed my soul. I had not felt so energized since I used to go for my chilly morning swims.

"Almost there, boy," I said as the black sandy beach came into view. "Five, four, three, two, one..."

We jumped out into the moist black grains I had not touched in forever, grounded the boat, and ran toward the dry sand and our saving grace up the hill ahead.

"Help me grab some of these diamonds," I said as I plucked them from the giving slopes of the mountain. A cornucopia of life-saving jewels, ours for the picking.

Silver grabbed three diamonds in his mouth, jogged over to me and placed them at my feet. I rewarded him with a hearty pat and ruffled his fur.

"Good boy, Silver. Thank you." He wagged his white-tipped tail and ran off to gather more stones. I placed as many as I could in my pockets until they were full. I pulled the front of my shirt from my dungarees, held it out with one hand and began filling it with the precious jewels.

"I didn't think about bringing something to put all of these in." I walked around the pristine mountain slopes, looking for something to use as a container. Stumbling on a rock, a few of the gems escaped and skittered off my snow boots. *Bingo!* I sat down on the black sandy slope, tugged the boots off my feet and began to fill them with as many diamonds as they could hold.

Silver whined, nudging my feet with his cold nose.

"I'll be okay, boy. Remember, I used to do this every winter morning in my bare feet."

We continued to scour the hills, filling the boots to the brim with diamonds.

"I think we've got all we can carry on this trip. Let's go."

CHAPTER 20

"Are you crazy?" Clay shrieked. Murph looked up from an empty soup can, spoon in hand.

"I need your help siphoning fuel from the bus to the emissaries' plane," I yelled as I ran barefoot through town, my feet barely registering the cold snow underfoot.

"That gasoline is all we have left," Clay said. "I won't help you steal it just to go flying around in that silly plane. And Lou, why are you barefoot?"

"Read this." I thrust the newspaper into his hand and pointed to the article. Murph read over his shoulder.

"I'm flying down to San Francisco to sell these diamonds and bring us back as many supplies as that Japanese plane will hold." I could barely contain my excitement. "We are going to be okay!"

"You know, it just might work," Murph said, tapping his jaw with the spoon. "Here, take my boots. We're about the same size. Go on. What are you waiting for?"

I gave him the biggest hug I could muster and slipped on his warm winter boots. They fit like a glove.

Murph and Silver jumped aboard the bus just as Clay tried to fire up the ornery thing for the first time since Jimmy left.

"It can't be that different from ole man Granger's tractor, can it now," Clay said, flipping levers and pumping the gas pedal.

The bus roared to life, and we sped up the hill toward the lake, slipping and sliding a bit on patches of snow and ice along the way.

"When we get there, I'll run get some tubing from Papa's shed. I'll see if he has a jug or something we can put the fuel in to transfer it to the plane. Murph, you get the bus ready. Clay, you get the plane ready."

"Now that's the Lou we all know and love. Back to giving orders. Aye-aye Capt'n Lou," Murph joked. I gave him a playful swat on the back of his head.

"Ow," he howled, much louder than was necessary. It was nice to mess around with my friends again.

Clay pulled the bus as close to the lake as he could and cut the engine as I ran for the shed. The tubing was nestled behind mops, brooms, and an old red wagon. Looking around, I saw a ceramic white tub Mama used to bathe me in when I was a baby. "That is one old tub," I laughed, grabbing it and a piece of tubing almost ten feet long. I tossed it into the tub, put them in the wagon, and pulled my stash back down the hill.

Murph had the tank ready at the bus, and Clay was working on the plane, changing out the battery with the one from the bus, opening the fuel tank, and emptying some water that had invaded the pontoons underneath it.

"I'll do the sucking, Lou," Murph said. He lowered one end of the tubing deep into the gasoline tank of the bus. I held the other end near the opening of the jug.

"Thanks, Murph. I never did like the taste of fuel," I said, laughing. It felt good to laugh and joke with him. It had been such a long, long time. I almost felt human again.

I handed him the other end. "On three. One, two, three..."

Murph stuck the tube in his mouth and took a deep breath in, sucking the fuel from the bottom of the tank up the black rubber tube. Just before the fuel reached his lips, he placed his tongue and then his finger over the tube's opening in his mouth and swung the tube into the tub. Our hearts raced as we heard the first trickle of fuel moving from the bus to the tub. We let the science of siphoning do its thing as we danced around the tub, twirling and giggling.

"Do you need anything else? A co-pilot maybe?"

"Thanks, Murph, but I think I need to go alone. That way, I can bring back more supplies." Murph pulled the wagon down the hill the final few feet to the dock as I stabilized the back end of it to keep the fuel from sloshing out too much. Silver stayed back about five feet. Smart dog.

"What about that red dot, Lou?" Clay said. "I don't think you should fly with that thing showin'."

Looking at the plane, I realized he had a very good point. "You're right. I sure wouldn't want to get shot down as the enemy. I think I saw some paint in the shed. Would you please go grab it?"

Clay high tailed it to find the paint and hopefully some brushes. With a grin the size of Texas, he ambled back down the hill to the lake as the last of the fuel siphoned into the plane's gas tank.

"Looky what I found," he smirked. Before me he held out five cans of paint: a yellow can, a mint green can, and three pink cans.

"Are you serious? You mean you couldn't even find a nice deep blue or gray?" I chirped.

"I guess your old man was going to paint something for your ma," he laughed.

"Well, one thing's for sure," I said. "We have to break up the shape of this plane with the paint or else I'll be spotted as Japanese for sure. I have the plane spotting chart in the tower. Be back in a jiffy."

"While you're at it," Clay added, "You might want to put on something a little more frilly, you know, in case you have to use your feminine wiles."

Murph nodded in agreement, crossing his arms and eyeing my less-than-fancy work duds.

"Very funny, you two." I glanced down at my dungarees with more holes than should be allowed. They were right. "I'll run into the house on the way back and put on something Mama would approve of."

"Well, let's get to work," Clay said. He and Murph painted the entire plane pink then he drew flowers along the wings, and painted "United States of America" in yellow with a green outline, on the fuselage.

Murph added pink and green stripes with yellow stars to try to emulate the US flag, then painted the tail number I gave him on the rudder in green.

"Wow," Murph said, whistling as I walked toward them in my Sunday-best embroidered winter-white wool dress, candy apple red cardigan sweater, and black shiny Mary Jane shoes.

"Well, it's not what Amelia would wear, but it's for a good cause," I added. "Nice job with the plane."

Holding up the spotting chart, I located the emissaries' plane. We looked from the drawing to our plane back and forth at least ten times.

"Boys, I think you've done it," I said.

"It doesn't look like anything the Japanese would fly anymore, much less any red-blooded American male," Murph snickered.

"Say, do you have a map or something to get you to San Francisco?" Clay asked.

"Hmm. I didn't think about that. There aren't any left at the airport. I'll check the cockpit."

I climbed into the plane and rummaged through its contents. An empty drink can, a parachute, and a handheld radio littered the seats. I located a map, but unfortunately, it was filled with foreign words and strange looking characters.

"This won't do me any good," I said, sticking my head out of the plane. "Guess I'll just fly west to the coast, hang a left, and fly south 'til I get there. That way I'll be sure not to fly past 'Frisco."

"Good luck, Lou," Clay said. "We are all proud of you, you know. We wouldn't have survived this long without you."

Pride blossomed in my heart and a genuine smile graced my face. "Thanks Clay. You're the best friend a girl could have. You too, Murph. Now get this bird untied for me, point me toward Mount Callisto and give me a shove. I want to see those diamonds glistening below as I leave the valley."

"Yes ma'am, Capt'n Lou."

CHAPTER 21

I secured the boots full of diamonds with the harness in the passenger seat behind me and tucked the newspaper article gently between them. I shimmied into the cracked leather pilot seat and shoved the useless map back in the pocket strapped to the inside of the plane. The plane smelled stale and old, like it had been simmering in motor oil. I straightened my lopsided skirt underneath me and opened the canopy an inch to get some fresh air while I figured out how to fly the metal bird.

"I need a few minutes to get familiar with the control panel."

"I'd need a couple of years," Murph chuckled.

"Here goes nothing," I said as I closed the door to the past and prepared to face the future. The town's future. My future. Fears attempted to surface, given the length of time it had been since I'd been in a cockpit. The fact that I'd never flown a Japanese plane started to concern me. All the labels were in gobbledygook. I couldn't read or make out anything. What if this plane worked differently than American planes? What if I'd forgotten everything I'd learned? What if I crashed and never got to San Francisco? What would happen to the kids?

I propped my head against the instrument panel for a moment and tried to steady my erratic breathing. *Be brave, Lou. It's all up to you now,* I thought. *You know what you have to do, so just be done with it.*

I tried to remember my old checklist: avionics off, cabin heat on, carb heat off, oil cooler open, beacon on, strobes on, mags on, fuel valve on, brake test and hold. Well, maybe a pontoon test.

At least they used the same numbering system we did. Looking for an instrument with digits in the thousands, I found the altimeter dial. *I shouldn't be flying over about three thousand feet. Now where's the compass?* I searched the panel and finally found it near the bottom. It looked vaguely like the ones I was used to, so I ignored the characters and knew where to look for my directional heading. I'd start out to the west, then turn south when I reached the ocean.

The horizon indicator was harder to find. They had stuck it near the bottom of the panel. It would help me stay level especially if it started getting cloudy on the way to 'Frisco and the ground became hard to see. The air speed indicator would be helpful, but as long as I didn't stall, speed wasn't that important to me.

Next I found the fuel gauges—two by my left knee and four by my right. *Wow—six fuel tanks. It must cost a pretty penny to fill this thing up.* Nearest I could figure, the tanks were just over half full. *Hope that's enough to make San Francisco,* I thought.

There was a panel of switches that had to house the fuel switches and the lights.

"Clay. Murph. Can you tell me when the lights come on?"

"Sure thing Capt'n Lou," Murph said.

I flipped about ten switches before Clay gave me a thumbs up. Three more switches and all the lights were turned on. There was no way to know which switch alternated between fuel tanks. I needed to figure that out in flight or I might use too much from one wing's tanks and not be able to switch to the others.

I licked my finger and stuck it outside the canopy to feel the wind. *Perfect! From the west, just like I'd hoped.*

"I think that's it. The only thing I can't find is how to start it. I'm used to a key, but I can't find a keyhole anywhere, much less a key. There are a couple of buttons and knobs. Maybe one of them is the starter. Only one way to find out."

Pulling the canopy most of the way closed, I yelled out, "*Clear!*"

Murph and Clay gave me a thumbs up from the dock. I returned the gesture. I pushed the first of the two buttons. Nothing. I turned the knob next to them and the engine tried to start. I pushed the throttle in and pulled the stick toward my body. The plane lurched forward. A scream screeched outside the plane, and I saw Murph cover his face as Clay pointed in front of me. The engine roared and stumbled, and I realized the plane was going to nosedive into the lake.

The throttle must be set in too far. Pull back.

Before I could get the throttle pulled back all the way, my throat closed off. *Not again. Not now.*

My face fell forward as the plane jerked back. My neck made a cracking noise and reversed course, my head flying back past where the headrest should have been. Struggling to catch my breath, I tried not to panic, but soon I felt like a fish out of water. I heard a high pitched wheeze and didn't know if it was from me or the plane. Feeling like the plane was imploding on me, I grabbed for the lock and unlatched the canopy, pushing it back with my last amount of strength. The propeller blew wind straight into my face.

If only I could breathe in some of that air. Maybe if I imagine the air going in, it will. I closed my eyes and visualized the air plunging into my lungs. In and out. In and out. I wasn't going to make it. The town wasn't going to make it. I was going to be a failure. I glanced back toward the dock and saw a splash of yellow. Becky was jumping up and down, waving and smiling.

You have to pull yourself together, Lou. She's hungry and depending on you. You have to make it to San Francisco for her and the others. You have to conquer this. Now. I turned back toward the mountain in front of me and closed my eyes, willing the asthma away. After another minute of coughing, I began sneezing.

That's odd. I've never had that happen before. The sneezes kept coming. After about the twentieth one, my breathing returned to normal. The sneezes must have pushed the old air out of my lungs enough to allow the new air in.

I held up a hand and waved to the well-wishers who had gathered on the dock and then pulled the canopy shut and latched it. Being a little more careful with the throttle, I pushed it in a centimeter at a time, just enough to get a feel for the effect on speed.

Sputtering out into the lake, I noticed intermittent frozen chunks of ice floating like heavy clouds in the water. It was a good thing the sun picked that day to peek through the clouds and shine on our valley again and that the temperature rose since the freezing pre-dawn hours. I thought I could take off safely, although who knew. I'd never taken off in a plane with pontoons before.

Back to my checklist. What's next? Oh yes. Avionics on. Taxi lights, nav lights and defrost on. I turned the plane's nose gear, well, pontoons, straight into the wind, for my run-up. *Are you supposed to run-up a seaplane? Time to find out.*

Compass? Check. Controls? Check. Fuel? Check, thanks to Murph and Clay. Canopy secured? Check. I realized I was holding my breath and began to feel a little woozy.

Okay, Lou. Breathe? Check. Breathe again? Check. Okay. Here goes nothing.

The plane began to glide gently across the still lake waters. The left pontoon skidded over a chunk of ice, momentarily tilting the plane to the right before it splashed down into the water.

Breathe, Lou. Breathe.

Building speed, I pulled back on the stick.

Liftoff.

I used full flaps and raised them when I climbed to about three-hundred feet above the water.

Just keep it steady, Lou. You can do this.

A gust whipped through the valley and over the lake, catching the wings. The plane reacted and dipped toward the water. My stomach lurched as I fought to keep the wings level. The left wingtip sliced through a wave just as I regained control.

Just a little bit further. That's it. Rise above the lake, plane. Up a little further. A little further. That's good.

Glancing at the altimeter, I determined I was about fifteen hundred feet up. I banked south just as I approached Mount Callisto, glancing down to see newly emerged diamonds shimmering below, wishing me well. Soon I would be over the ridge and could find some smoother air.

San Francisco, here I come.

CHAPTER 22

The Pacific Ocean glistened and gleamed beneath me as I turned the plane toward the east and flew over the Golden Gate Bridge. The suspension bridge stood as tall as a giant, welcoming me to 'Frisco Bay. I remembered going there as a child with Mama and Papa before the war. We took a boat by the island of Alcatraz and saw the federal prison standing sentinel on top of it. Looking down, I could just make it out in the middle of the bay ahead of me. Goose bumps covered my arms as I remembered the infamous Al Capone was housed there last time I was here. During that trip, we visited the terminus of the transcontinental railway, saw a performance of the San Francisco Opera, boated by the man-made Treasure Island, and visited some of the old gold mines. Funny how people in the eighteen hundreds came here to find their fortunes, and here I was, nearly one hundred years later, to cash in on Claret Lake's.

Just before flying by Alcatraz, I made a radio call to announce my arrival to whoever was listening on the radio waves.

"San Francisco air traffic, this is Love Oboe Uncle One Six, over." That was as good a tail number to make up as any. And easy to remember: my name and my age.

A gruff voice responded. "Love Oboe Uncle One Six, what is your destination? And what kind of plane are you flying?"

"Love Oboe Uncle One Six is destined for J.G. Brothers Manufacturing, Pier Eight, the Embarcadero. Love Oboe Uncle One Six is an American plane from Lagune County, California."

"Proceed, Love Oboe Uncle One Six. Winds are at twenty from the west. Stay southwest of Treasure Island."

"Winds are twenty from the west," I repeated. "Proceeding southwest of Treasure Island. Love Oboe Uncle One Six."

Whew! I made it through the radio call. Good thing we took that boat trip when we were here before. Otherwise, I wouldn't have known Treasure Island from Alcatraz. I relaxed for the first time in hours, enjoying the bird's-eye view of San Francisco from above for a few glorious seconds. Feeling free as a falcon, I saw piers jutting out into the sparkling waters of the bay, cable cars straining to make it to the top of the steepest streets in the city, and in the middle of it all were people playing golf like they were oblivious that a war was raging beyond the shores.

Glancing behind me for air traffic, I saw the daily blanket of fog just beginning its trek into the bay, rolling in from the ocean. It looked like I arrived just in time. Another hour and I wouldn't have been able to land. I banked the plane to the right of Treasure Island and saw piers in the distance just over my starboard wing. I decided to fly over them first and locate the J.G. Brothers manufacturing plant on Pier Eight before I landed.

Scanning the numerous piers jutting into the bay, I started counting. *One, two, three, four, five, six, seven, eight. There! That has to be it!*

It looked like there was a loading dock I could tie up to after I landed. I began to bank the plane and turned around to enter my landing pattern when I saw a plane fly between me and the pier.

The pilot held up his radio and pointed to it, motioning for me to talk to him.

I looked down and found I had inadvertently switched off the radio when I tossed it onto my lap.

Pressing the call button, I said, "Love Oboe Uncle One Six here."

"Love Oboe Uncle One Six, this is the United States Navy. You are instructed to land on Treasure Island, Runway Two-Five, immediately."

"But sir, I need to land at J.G. Brothers Manufacturing at Pier Eight. Love Oboe Uncle One Six."

"Love Oboe Uncle One Six, if you do not turn around immediately and land at Treasure Island, I will be forced to fire on you."

"But..."

"Do you really want to crash into the bay, or is that what you Japs like to do?"

"I'm not a..."

"Three... Two..."

"Okay! Okay! I'm going," I screamed.

I banked to the left and followed his lead. As I approached the runway, I switched the lever I assumed would put the landing gear down. *Horsefeathers!* I didn't think I had any landing gear, only pontoons. I got on the radio one more time.

"Um, sir? This is Love Oboe Uncle One Six. I don't think I have any wheels. May I land in the water by that dock over there?"

After what seemed like an eternity, I heard some voices through the static. "Proceed to Dock Seventeen on the west side of the island and await the AG's. I will escort you there. *Do not*, I repeat, *do not* exit the plane."

"Proceed to Dock Seventeen on the west side of the island and wait for the AG's. Do not exit the plane. Got it. Love Oboe Uncle One Six."

CHAPTER 23

Navy Armed Guards with automatic machine guns approached the pink, green, and yellow plane. Their lips quivered, and I could tell some of them were doing everything in their power *not* to laugh. One young AG lost control, and he bent double as his chuckle escaped. He received a thwack on the back of the head from the guy next to him. I put on my prettiest smile and waved to them through the grimy window. A couple of AG's tentatively returned the wave.

"Please open the canopy, ma'am," the lieutenant said.

"Sure thing, sir," I replied, sitting in the plane.

He extended his large, weathered hand toward me, acting every bit the gentleman I am sure he was.

I kept my hands inside the plane, looked him squarely in his big green eyes and said, "The kind gentleman in the plane that escorted me here told me, and I quote, '*Do not*, I repeat, *do not* exit the plane,' so I am not sure I should get out until he tells me it's okay." I blinked my most innocent baby blues up at him and flashed him a matching smile. The men lost it at that moment and laughter rolled across the dock like the waves in the ocean just past the Golden Gate.

"I can assure you, young lady, that it *is* okay. I am the base commander's right-hand man, and he gives that pilot's orders as well as mine."

"Well then, I guess I can get out." Grabbing the boots full of diamonds and the newspaper, I clutched them close against my chest with one hand and took his hand with the other. I exited the plane, stepping gingerly onto the dock and quickly got my land legs back. At least I was safely on terra firma again. Kind of.

"Are you American?" he asked.

"Of course, I'm American. Don't I look it?" I said in the most astonished voice I could muster.

He led me by the elbow down the dock with five armed guards.

We climbed fifty-two steps—I counted them—to reach headquarters. It had been a beautiful day, but the fog had almost encased Treasure Island by now. *How will I ever find J.G Brothers in this pea soup?*

We marched down a narrow sidewalk lined with pear trees. They looked like the ones we harvested in the fall, only bigger, and greener. A whitewashed building boasting window boxes overflowing with red geraniums and blue hydrangeas awaited our arrival.

148

"Stand down," the lieutenant said to a guard at the main entrance. He opened the door and motioned for me to enter. The other escorts behind us dropped their weapons, bounded down the stairs and returned to their posts, laughing and slapping each other on the back along the way. The lieutenant rolled his eyes and led me by the elbow to an interrogation room just past the reception desk. A pretty red-head winked at the navy man, and he tipped his hat to her.

"I'll let him know he has a visitor in Interrogation Room One, Lieutenant Marshall," she said with a knowing smile.

"Thank you, Cathy," he replied, trying to suppress his grin.

Lieutenant Marshall opened a heavy metal door that grated on the floor.

"Sit down in that chair there, ma'am," he said. "The base commander will be along shortly."

"Thank you ever so much, sir," I said, holding my boots close to my chest and sitting in what looked to be the least comfortable chair in the room. *Maybe if the commander has the more comfortable one, I can get through this sooner and get on to J. G. Brothers.*

I let out a pent-up breath and clung tightly to the boots that held my lifeline. Claret Lake's lifeline.

To my surprise, the base commander entered the interrogation room with three more armed guards.

I rose from the uncomfortable seat, extended one hand and said, "Hello, sir, I'm ..."

"Why are you flying a Japanese plane?" he interrupted, slamming his hands down on the dingy green metal desk separating us. I sat down with a thud.

"Well, it's a long story, sir," I said, running my nervous hands down the supple leather of the diamond-laden boots. "But you see, just over two years ago, some Japanese emissaries landed in Claret Lake north of here. That's where I'm from—Claret Lake. Up in Lagune County? Anyway, there was too much fog here in San Francisco for them to land, so they went north and ended up on our lake. They were on their way to Washington D.C., so since they had to detour, D.C. sent a different plane to escort them for the rest of their journey. This plane here, their plane, sat at my mama and papa's dock for the past two years with a blasted big red dot on it."

I looked around at the men who were fidgeting. They didn't look very comfortable seeing a young girl interrogated. Either that or they didn't like listening to a female recount the long version of a story. But I didn't want to end up in the brig, so I figured I should tell the commander the entire tale. I had to get to J.G. Brothers to sell the diamonds so I could get back to Claret Lake with the food and supplies we desperately needed.

"Please continue, Miss..."

"Lucinda Davis. But please call me Lou."

"Alright, Lou. Continue." He crossed his burly arms and flexed his biceps. They must have had a heck of a gym around there somewhere. He looked like he could break me in two with his pinkie finger.

"So the next thing that happened is that the census bureau had made a mistake in 1940 and showed our county had a population of four-hundred thousand, not the actual forty thousand we had. The draft board took every boy and every man over eighteen years old to the war. Everyone except for Doc, and he's, let's see, he should be about ninety-seven by now. Even the navy didn't want him."

That garnered a snicker and a couple of strange sneezes out of the armed men blocking the door.

"And then all the womenfolk, my mama included, had to go to Richmond to get jobs building ships to support the war effort. But we kids couldn't go with them, so they left us behind to run the town."

"Yeah, right," one of the men coughed under his breath.

"It's *true*," I cried, turning toward him. "And they left *me* in charge, and it's been a total disaster. We are out of food and out of supplies. I was at the end of my rope when Rex, the Indian chief—I'm a member of the tribe, but that's another story—sat with me and talked in all kinds of riddles like he always does. But when he left,

I figured it all out. We have these diamonds on the slopes of the mountain across the lake. See?" I set the boots on the table to show him the contents. The commander fingered them and cocked his head at me.

"No fooling?" he questioned.

"No fooling," I replied. "Anyway, Silver and I, that's my dog, collected as many as we could, and I flew down here to sell them to J. G. Brothers so I can buy supplies and food for the kids. See this article here?" I showed the commander the newspaper and pointed to the article. "That's why I'm here. But to finish my story, there were no planes left behind when all the men went to war except for this one. I knew I couldn't fly into San Francisco in a Japanese plane with a big red dot on it, and I needed to break up the shape of the plane a little visually, so my friends and I found the only paint we could in my papa's shed. And you can see the results for yourself."

"I must admit, young lady, the paint did have us fooled until one of our plane spotters saw the actual shape as you passed Treasure Island. I need to check a few facts, but after I clear your story, you may proceed on your mission. How long have you been a pilot?"

"Golly, I'm not technically a pilot. I've never even soloed until today. Before the war, some of my papa's hunting buddies had pilots fly them around, and in their off time, they would take me up and teach me a thing or

152

two. I'm a quick study, especially when it's something I really care about, like flying. I've always wanted to be a pilot, like Amelia Earhart, so I listened closely and learned as much as I could. Sometimes they would let me take the stick for a bit, and one even let me land a plane once. But when all the men left, so did all the planes, and I haven't flown since. Until today."

"Hmm," he muttered, tapping his pencil eraser on the cold metal table between us. "Interesting tale. Well, you stay here while I check into a few things. My name is Captain Hill. Would you like a soda pop?" he offered.

"Oh boy, would I ever! That would be swell! And sir, do you by chance have any chocolate bars?"

With a bar of chocolate in my pocket, one in my stomach, and the diamond-filled boots and newspaper clutched to my chest, I walked back toward my pink, green and yellow plane escorted by Captain Hill himself.

"Just so we're clear, we've added Love Oboe Uncle One Six to our list of valid tail numbers. Very clever, by the way. If anyone gives you a problem, have them call me directly here at Treasure Island. I must say, you are one impressive young lady. My sources say you have done a bang-up job keeping that town going."

"Thank you, sir," I said, enjoying the scent of the humid, salty air as we reached the dock, wondering who his sources could possibly be.

"You will leave your plane right where it is until you are ready to leave San Francisco, which should be within twenty-four hours, mind you. While you are in my jurisdiction, I am assigning an ensign to escort you via boat to J. G. Brothers and to any supply stores you plan on patronizing."

"Thank you again, sir. I will make it snappy."

My Mary Jane's clicked and clacked on the dock as we approached a handsome, perfectly postured ensign standing sentinel by my colorful plane. He saluted the commander who returned the tradition. Captain Hill turned and retreated to the base. I stared at the ensign for a moment, then butterflies appeared unexpectedly in my stomach and suddenly began aerobatic flight maneuvers. Placing my hand on my belly, I willed them to calm down.

He's just a guy, Lou. A dreamy one, yes, but still just a guy. Now get a grip. You have a town to save.

The butterflies didn't agree.

When my feet decided to move again, I took a deep breath and approached him, extending my trembling right hand, the boots securely clutched with my left.

The ensign wore his hat low and shifted his hands to his hips. The single gold bars riding high atop each shoulder glinted in the sun. I could tell he was glaring at me behind his reflective sunglasses underneath that formal white hat. He probably had more important things to be doing than coddling a girl. Well, it wasn't my fault the base commander ordered him to escort me. Even so, I figured it was up to me to break the ice.

"Hello, I'm..."

"I know who you are, Lou," the ensign quipped. He reached up and removed his white hat and sunglasses. "Don't you recognize me?"

CHAPTER 24

"*Jimmy!*" I screamed, dropping my boots, running and leaping into his outstretched arms. I wrapped my legs around him like a kid clinging to her childhood hero.

"I can't believe it's you!" I kissed his right cheek, then his left, and then started all over again. "Oh my, you're a sight for sore eyes! What are you doing here?" I hugged him with all of my might. I didn't ever want to let go.

He twirled me around and gently returned me to the ground, although my spirit would soar for the rest of the week, I was sure of it.

"Escorting you, of course," he replied with a wink, a twinkle in his eye, and the most fabulous smile I had seen in forever.

"Your hair is so short!" I laughed and ran my hand through his quarter-inch locks. It may have been short, but it was as soft as silk to my fingertips.

"All this time, and that's all you can say?" he replied.

"Oh, Jimmy!" I put my arms around him again and decided that indeed, I was not going to let him go for a very long time. Hugging him felt the closest I'd felt to home since all the craziness started. The scent of his aftershave lingered in the breeze, and the starch from his perfectly pressed white uniform tickled my nose. He broke away from my hold, looking down at me with the darkest chocolate brown eyes I'd ever seen. Chocolate never looked so tempting, so delicious, so inviting.

"Now, ma'am, where would you like to go?" He bowed in front of me, pausing on his way back up to flash me a roguish grin. "I'm at your service for the next twenty-four hours."

I shook my head and tried with all my might to make sure it wasn't a dream.

"Jimmy, I just can't believe it. You're actually here. It just about killed me when you had to leave. You were my rock after Papa went away. I could always depend on you. You know, that blasted school bus has acted up ever since you left. I think it misses you more than I do."

"The war has kept me busy," he said, staring into the distance, looking like the weight of the world had just settled on his shoulders. Shaking his head, he drew his gaze back to my face. "I'm actually on leave today and was on my way to Oakland. But when I saw you hop out of that awful looking plane, I knew I had to stick around and see you. The base really can't spare anyone to babysit you, so I volunteered."

I put my hands on my hips and glared at him, trying to feign indignity. "I do *not* need babysitting, Ensign Jimmy," I said, emphasizing it with a stomp of one Mary Jane. "I can take care of myself. And by the way, thanks for all those newsy letters."

"Now hold on, Pipsqueak." He leaned in closer, placed his hands on my shoulders, and gave me a kiss on my blushing cheek. "I'm just joking, Lou, and you know it. And I'm sorry I haven't had a chance to write, but I've missed you."

My arms automatically found their place around his waist, and he returned the favor. My cheek rested on his capable shoulder. There was no doubt he had grown into quite a man over the past few months. Muscles that were never visible before had emerged along with an air of self-confidence that only the military can provide.

"I've missed you, too. Terribly. All of us have." I pulled back and smiled up at him. "Just wait until I tell Clay and Murph that I had my own personal navy escort in 'Frisco. They'll just die!"

His signature chuckle resonated with my butterflies. I couldn't help but smile at him.

A seagull swooped overhead sounding its usual cry. It buzzed the pink, yellow and green plane, mistaking it for the mother of all flowers, and then turned south to cross the bay.

"Let's get this show on the road, or on the water, as the case may be," Jimmy said. "Where to, m' lady?"

I giggled at his formality. Who knew joining the navy would make Jimmy into such a gentleman? I couldn't help but remember racing down the dirt road to school with him, skipping stones, him pulling my hair in class and pretending he didn't do it. And him chiding me about wanting to be a pilot, seeing as I'm a girl and all.

"J. G. Brothers, please, sir. I believe it's southwest on Pier Eight," I said, thrusting my shoulders back and saluting him, standing as tall as humanly possible. Even so, he towered over me now, blocking the sun from my eyes.

My, how many inches has he grown?

"Then that's where I shall take you, m' lady. Care to take my hand?"

I placed my small one, worn beyond its years by work in the fields, delicately into his strong, capable one. A wave must have struck the dock because my knees all of a sudden felt like they were giving way on me. Maybe it was a tremor, or a small earthquake. It was California after all. I stumbled a bit when stepping into the boat, and Jimmy quickly braced my elbow, putting his other hand around my waist. I smiled what felt like a feeble smile, looking up into his welcoming gaze.

159

"I'll just grab your stash, and then we'll be ready to go."

I had forgotten all about the diamonds sprawled out on the deck. They scattered in every direction when I dropped the boots. For several wonderful, glorious minutes, the worries of the world had jumped from my shoulders and run away. I had completely forgotten why I had come to San Francisco in the first place.

Immediately I clamored ungracefully out of the boat and crawled on my hands and knees to help him round up the escapees. We each filled a boot until a few stragglers were all that were left. Our hands brushed as we both reached for the final diamond at the same time. A warm jolt of electricity invaded my body at his touch. It must have hit Jimmy, too, because he looked up at me while he grasped my hand with his.

"I'm glad you're here, Lou."

"Me, too, Jimmy. Me, too." We each grabbed a boot and set them on the dock next to the boat. He extended a hand to help me in. I stepped down into the craft and turned back toward him as he handed me the first boot.

"There's a supply box under that bench seat there," he said. "Just take off the lid. You should be able to place the boots inside it."

Turning toward the bench, I saw a metal tub with the navy seal printed on the side. Lifting off the lid, I shimmied the boot into an opening between the supplies and made room for the second one. The boat jostled slightly as Jimmy stepped in, grabbed the second boot and handed it to me. I nestled it next to the other one and replaced the lid to protect the jewels during the ride.

"Why don't you sit here by me, Lou," he said, patting the spot beside him. I tried to delicately lower myself onto the bench but miscalculated the distance and ended up on my fanny in a puddle on the floor of the boat. I felt my face flush. It was probably as bright as the red dot we painted over on the emissaries' plane.

Jimmy leapt to my side and knelt in the puddle without a thought for his perfectly pressed uniform. "Are you okay, Lou? Here, hold onto me."

I grabbed his thick, muscular arms and wondered once again how he could have grown into a full-fledged man in such a short amount of time. He spread a towel with 'US Navy' emblazoned on it over the bench. This time I paid more attention to where I was going and settled in for the ride across the bay.

Jimmy kept smiling at me, and for all the tea in China, I couldn't take my eyes off of him.

We sped across the choppy afternoon waters of San Francisco Bay. Sea spray pelted our faces, and the smell of salty seawater assaulted our senses. The wind whipped my hair around my face as we laughed and pretended we were out for a joy ride on Claret Lake. I closed my eyes and relished in the feeling, the wonderful sensation, of being taken care of for a few wonderful hours by someone I trusted beyond words. Trusted with my life. I allowed myself to let my guard down. Allowed myself to feel human again.

Jimmy slowed the boat as we entered a no-wake zone signaling our approach to Pier Eight. I opened my eyes and caught him staring at me. He took one hand from the steering wheel and tucked a stray blonde strand behind my ear. It seemed like an eternity passed before he broke his gaze.

"I think I see it," he said quietly, pointing toward a dingy gray building behind me, almost engulfed in the heavily hanging clouds. "Just up there. I'll pull aside the dock and secure the boat."

My head nodded in agreement, but my voice wouldn't cooperate. I swallowed a lump in my throat and hoped it didn't kill the butterflies in my stomach. I was beginning to like having them there, flying around and increasing my awareness of this familiar, yet new person taking such good care of me.

Jimmy swung the boat into place and cut the engine. He was out of the craft and had it deftly secured before I had a chance to offer any help. Then he extended his hand to help me to shore.

"Thank you, Jimmy." I barely got the whisper to escape my lips.

"My pleasure, Lou." He gently held me by the arms, then pulled his hands a mere inch away, watching me all the while to make sure I had my footing before he left my side.

"Stay right here, and I'll get the diamonds for you."

CHAPTER 25

Staring up at the mammoth, dark steel doors of J. G. Brothers Manufacturing, I rubbed my hands down the sides of my dress, trying to dry the sweat from them and at the same time, attempting to straighten out some of the wrinkles from the trip. It felt like Judgment Day. Either I got to enter the pearly gates and reap all the rewards Heaven can offer, or I would be banished to an eternity of fire and brimstone.

Jimmy put his arm around me and briefly lowered his lips to mine, leaving me breathless. Then he swung the heavy door open as deftly as if it were made of tule reeds.

"Here goes nothing," I whispered, staring into the abyss ahead of us.

We walked down a corridor lined with all types of interesting pieces of machinery and goods.

"J. G. Brothers must make everything from ball bearings to bathtubs," I said. "There must be a thousand things in this one hall alone."

We approached a cute receptionist with short, curly blonde locks. She tilted her head and gave Jimmy the once over and a more than approving smile.

I rolled my eyes. *Oh, please. How obvious can she be?*

And then to my surprise, Jimmy leaned down, rested one elbow on her desk, a hand on his hip, and crossed his right shiny black shoe over his left. Taking his hat off, he gave her a sly smile.

"Hello gorgeous," he said in a deep drawl. "Who's in charge of this place?"

She batted her mascara-laden lashes at him. "My, you're a good-looking ensign. Who might I say is asking?

"Jim Hastings, United States Navy," he said.

I nudged him, but he swatted my hand away.

"I'll see what I can do, Jim Hastings, United States Navy," she purred.

She picked up the phone receiver and turned her chair to face the wall while she talked to someone on the other end.

I pulled Jimmy away from the desk and growled, "What was that all about?"

He leaned down and whispered. "Just play along, Lou. I'm trying to get you in to see the head honcho. So what if I have to use my masculine wiles." He waggled his eyebrows and briefly looked like the Jimmy I knew and loved again. *Now where did the "L-word" come from?*

"Mr. Brothers will see you now," the bleach-blonde said, tapping Jimmy on the shoulder and tucking a card into the palm of his hand, curling his manly fingers over it with her perfectly manicured, feminine ones. "Just down that hall there, third door on the left, Sugar."

Jimmy glanced down at the card before lifting her hand and planting a kiss on it.

"Thanks, Gladys, and thanks for, *everything*," he said, nodding toward the card in his hand.

I rolled my eyes and started walking down the long corridor.

Jimmy sprinted to catch up with me. "Why are you walking so fast?"

"I had to get away from the love-fest back there," I replied. "I was about to lose my lunch, if I'd eaten anything today." When had I actually last eaten? Oh yeah, the chocolate bar at the base. Funny, chocolate had never made me feel sick to my stomach before.

He laughed and pulled me close just outside the third door to the left.

"You're cute when you're jealous." He smiled as I stomped my foot, but then he turned serious, looking deep into my eyes. "Would you like me to go in there with you, Lou?"

"Thanks Jimmy, but I can do this. I've come this far. And for your information, I am *not* jealous."

"Then good luck," he said, handing me the boots. "I'll be out checking on the boat. Just holler if you need me."

"Thanks, Jimmy. Maybe *Gladys* can keep you company."

"I only have eyes for you, Lou," he chuckled, leaning down to kiss me on the cheek. But just as he did, he turned and kissed me squarely on the lips. There must have been a power surge because my insides trembled and I was sure I saw sparks fly out of the lights above me.

A short man with a bow tie and just a wisp of hair on the top of his head breezed past us, clutching some papers and looking uncomfortable with our display of, well, whatever it was.

"Now go knock 'em dead, Pipsqueak," Jimmy said and opened the doors behind me. "Go save Claret Lake."

CHAPTER 26

I felt a cool whoosh of air as Jimmy shut the doors behind me. I walked in, full of confidence that my plan would work, but seeing the grimace on the heavily bearded face in front of me had me cowering by the time I reached a giant mahogany desk that would have filled my entire house back in Claret Lake. A hairy hand motioned to a leather chair that would seat Attila the Hun. I sank into it, sure that I had disappeared from his view.

"Who are you, and what do you want?" He growled between clenched teeth that held the last remnants of a stinky cigar.

Someone must have been having a worse day than me. "My name is Lou Davis, sir."

"Lou? That's no name for a girl. Besides, Gladys told me it was a, and I quote, 'Dreamy guy named Jim Hastings, United States Navy.'"

"Well, I may not be dreamy," I said, "and I'm certainly not a guy. Gladys must be bleaching her hair too much." I immediately clamped my hand over my mouth, realizing that I had actually said that out loud.

Mr. Brothers stood abruptly and slammed two furry mammoth paws down on the desk that trembled beneath his wrath. Then a laugh as deep as the Grand Canyon erupted.

"No one has ever gone up against Gladys, young lady," he laughed. "I like someone with spunk. So why are *you* here?"

"Well, Mr. Brothers, I am here to sell you two boots full of diamonds." I placed the boots on his desk as forcefully as his fists, and a few of the gems jumped out to greet him.

"My, my," he said with a gleam in his eye. He grabbed a pair of glasses and then a diamond and ran a rough finger over its faceted sides. I tried to gather the stones that jumped ship, but his hand waved mine away.

"Where did you get all these rocks, Cookie?" he asked, his right brow rising, allowing the evil eye back into his gaze. "Did you steal them?"

"I certainly did *not* steal them!" I spit out, angry that anyone could accuse me of something so horrible. "I found them on a mountain near where I live, and I need to sell them to save our town. You see, there was a mess up in the census in our county and because of it, all the men had to go to war and all the women had to go to Richmond to build ships. They left me and Jimmy, or

'Jim Hastings, United States Navy,' in charge, but when he turned eighteen, he was drafted, too. So now it's just me, and things are not going well. We are out of food and out of supplies, and if I don't get some money to buy what we need, we kids are all going to starve to death."

"Hmm," he muttered, moving to my side of the desk and running his eyes up and down my Sunday best.

Not sure that he was listening to me, I raised my voice a few decibels and tried to shift out of his reach. "Look, sir, are you interested in the diamonds or not?" I pulled the wrinkled, worn piece of newsprint from deep in my pocket and slapped it on the table in front of him. "This newspaper article says you are." I pointed to it, and he glanced at the article's title. Skimming the content, he grabbed a handful of diamonds and let them trickle through his fingers onto the antique desk.

"I'll give you fifty clams for the lot." He stroked his hairy hand up and down my arm and pulled me forcefully toward him, stroking a crooked finger down the curve of my face. I was sure I felt steam coming from my ears and wondered if that could really happen. I had come all this way, knowing the moon tears would save us. And for what?

"Fifty measly dollars?" I heard my voice squeak as I struggled to get away, but he was five times my size and twelve times as strong. I tried to scream, but he held me harder. He grabbed my arm like a human tourniquet, and I began to get scared.

As he clenched his teeth, he whispered, "You *will* sell them to me for fifty measly, as you call them, dollars." He reached for a folder on the desk behind with his free hand and withdrew a piece of paper on which he wrote "Fifty dollars for two boots full of diamonds."

"Now don't let out one little scream, or you will really be sorry. Sign here." He forced a pen into my trembling hand and pulled my fist toward the paper.

A bill of sale? How can this be happening? Where did I go wrong? All I wanted was to sell the diamonds for enough to buy supplies, then get back to Claret Lake.

My arm shook as I struggled to pull away from him. The harder I fought, the more he clamped down on my wrist. I tried to breathe, but my asthma took over and sucked all the air out of the room. My throat closed, and I fought to inhale—just one breath.

Knowing he wouldn't stop hurting me until I signed the paper, I looked around to see if there was anything I could use to defend myself or at least get in a good slug. Staring down at the desk, I saw the edge of a letter opener peeking out from under one of my boots.

He grabbed my hair and held it tight, jerking my head from side to side with his nasty right paw, clasping one lone diamond and crushing it into my skull. The other one squeezed my right arm. Using my free hand, I lunged for the letter opener, grabbed the handle and raised it to the back of his neck. *One good swipe should do it.*

"*Ouch! Witch! Look what you've done!*" he screamed as he wiped the back of his neck and came up with blood. Still grasping my hair, the monster jerked my head back. I lifted the blade and sliced him again across the forearm.

He let loose and fell backward toward the desk. I broke free and twirled around, letter opener still in hand. Anger and adrenaline forged a way for me to breathe.

"You take one step toward me and I swear I'll slice you again. Now move away from the desk."

I put all the diamonds back in my boots and clutched them to my chest. "Fifty measly dollars? For *all* these diamonds? Are you *crazy*? You'll rot in Hades before I take fifty dollars for all of these." I looked at him, biting the inside of my cheek to regain my composure, not sure if the trickle of blood I tasted was inflicted by me or him. The angrier I became, the louder my voice belted, escalating and reverberating throughout the enormous room.

"I'll press charges and sue you for this," the monster growled. "You will *never* see the light of day again!"

"Are you sure you want to do that, sir?" Jimmy said in a voice as calm as the quiet before the nastiest of storms. "You have two witnesses that will attest otherwise."

We both turned toward the open doors to see Jimmy and Gladys standing in the doorway. With the fires of the entire war in his eyes, Jimmy marched toward us.

I held up my hand. "You stay right there, Jimmy. This is my fight."

Turning back toward the monster, I clenched my teeth and held up my weapon. "I'd rather be covered in honey and eaten by ants than to sign that paper. Rip it up. Right now."

The beast grunted and tore the page into pieces, crumpling them and throwing them on the floor by my feet.

I walked toward the door and handed Jimmy the boots. I looked up at the equal mixture of anger and concern in his eyes. He looked ready to attack, like he was filled with the full assault force of the entire United States Navy.

"Not yet," I whispered.

He stayed where he was as I turned to face the beast once more. Marching back toward the desk, I grabbed the diamond he still clutched in his right hand.

"I believe this is *my* property. I may be sixteen, but I am not stupid. I may be a girl, but I am not a quitter. I may be desperate, but I am not *that* desperate. I *will* find a buyer for these jewels, someone who is honest, unlike you, and will give me a good price, unlike you. It may take a while, but I'd rather starve than do business with the likes of an unethical, immoral cheater like you."

I turned to leave. "He's all yours," I said to Jimmy, handing him the letter opener. I took my boots and left the room.

Jimmy shut the massive doors behind me with the look of a man completely resolved to skin another alive.

"I'll be right back with a cold compress for your arm, honey," Gladys said, patting my shoulder. "You sure got gumption, Sugar. Don't know what your boyfriend can do that you haven't already."

"But he's not my..."

She turned and headed down the hallway, her heels clicking through the darkness.

Turning my ear to the crack between the doors, I strained to hear what was going on inside. All I could make out were low voices and an occasional curse. Jimmy's voice became a little louder as he approached the door.

"Is that clear?" he asked.

"Crystal," the monster replied.

"Good, and you might want to get a Tetanus shot for those wounds soon," Jimmy said, opening the doors as I failed at trying to look like I wasn't eavesdropping.

Jimmy shut the doors behind him. He grasped my shoulders and looked into my eyes. "Are you okay, Lou? Gladys was eavesdropping over the intercom and ran out to tell me what was happening. I wish I could have rescued you, but it looks like you'd already taken care of things yourself."

"Darn tootin'," I said, looking up, managing a weak smile.

"That sorry excuse for a man in there is a...well, it's not fit to say in front of a lady," Jimmy said. "But I can promise he will *never* hurt you again."

The enormity of what had happened hit me all at once as I looked at him. "Jimmy, I failed. I failed Claret Lake. I just knew this was the answer." My head dropped into my hands, and I felt the adrenaline rush disappear, along with my hopes of saving the town.

He held me close and wiped a spatter of blood from my arm with his perfectly starched handkerchief that soon matched his perfectly mussed uniform.

"Let's go, Jimmy," I said, taking his protective hand. My wrist began to show the start of several blooming bruises, and my skull throbbed.

Gladys met us at her desk. "I'm sorry you had to go through that, honey. Here, take this." She handed me a

175

cold compress and gently wiped my face with a cool cloth, surprising me with her genuine concern.

"Why do you think I flirt with all the good-looking men that come through here?" she said, glancing Jimmy's way. "All the women here get harassed by that monster every day, but we have to work to support our families during the war, so we don't have a choice. We've filed complaints, but so far, no help. And jobs are so scarce that we can't afford to quit. But I must say, none of us have half the courage that you do." She extended her hand to shake mine. "I'm honored to have made your acquaintance, Lou Davis. Good luck with your quest."

She walked back toward her desk like a lamb to the slaughter, and my jealousy melted as quickly as ice in the desert heat. Abruptly, she stopped and turned back toward us. "Hey, why don't you try Mr. Morales over on Jackson Street, Pier Five? He's a good man—an honest man. I'll give his secretary, Hilda, a call and let her know you and your handsome sailor are on your way."

CHAPTER 27

"We did it!" I screamed, running out of Morales Manufacturing, waving an envelope filled with more money than I had ever seen.

Jimmy sprinted toward me, and I jumped into his arms as he twirled me around Pier Five.

"Thanks to Gladys and Hilda, Mr. Morales bought every last diamond I brought for *one thousand dollars!*"

"You did it, Lou! I knew you could!" Jimmy smiled as he spun me one last time on the pier before placing my feet gently on the faded wooden planks weathered from years of exposure to salt water. He held his hands gently to my bruised arm and kissed it as if it were the most sacred thing on the planet. His eyes shifted up to mine as he said, "Now let's go shopping."

"Just what every girl wants to hear from her guy!" I said, nestling the envelope that would save Claret Lake into my front pocket, outlined in delicate winter-white lace and secured with a lone mother-of-pearl button.

"So I'm your guy, Lou?" he said, looking serious all of a sudden, and then turning on a grin that would light up Claret Lake on a cloudy, moonless night.

I skipped down the pier and turned, motioning for him to join me.

"Come on Ensign Jimmy, sir," I laughed. "Here's my list. Let's do some serious shopping!"

The street was teeming with every type of store imaginable: Woolworth's Five and Dime, butcher shops, bakeries, drug stores, flower stands, theaters, clothing stores, toy stores, liquor stores, smoke shops, and Mom and Pops everywhere. But mostly just the Moms seemed to be around.

The aroma of freshly baked bread wafted through the alleys. The smooth, sweet smell of cigar smoke drifted from a table where three elderly gentlemen wearing fedoras played a game of chess. People milled through the streets, some hawking their wares, others selecting fresh vegetables and succulent fruits from the markets for dinner.

Jimmy and I worked our way through my list, taking breaks to haul our purchases back to the boat at Jackson Street, Pier Five. Jimmy had moved the boat there while I met with Mr. Morales. Seems he felt I could take care of myself and didn't need him waiting right outside the door for that particular meeting.

I glanced into the boat filled with cans of food, bags of flour and sugar, slabs of cured meats, warm clothes, jackets, new boots, some ammunition for my bolt-action .22, and as much as I could shove in to keep Claret Lake going, hopefully for the duration of the war.

There wasn't much room for more than the essentials, but I tried to pick up something special for everyone back home: an antique brass magnifying glass for Doc, a grammar book for Aunt Mary, fashion magazines and a spatula set for Bev and Julie, and pocket knives for Clay, Murph, Ralph and Tommy. I found a box of foot long matches for Eddie, a horse magazine for Barbara, a writing journal for Fern, a locket for Becky, a bandana for Silver, fresh carrots for Bucky, and a leather knife pouch for Rex. I even managed to talk Jimmy into visiting Ghirardelli on North Point Street to sample and purchase several pounds of their legendary chocolate.

"Well, you certainly won't be running out of chocolate any time soon," Jimmy chuckled as we headed for the boat.

I took another bite of the creamy chocolaty treat. A grin as wide as the Golden Gate Bridge spread across my face.

"Do you think the plane can fly with all of this, Lou?" Jimmy asked, eyeing our haul with concern.

"I sure hope so. Everyone is going to be so excited to have warm clothes for the winter, sturdy shoes for the

179

snow, and an assortment of food for their bellies. And it's nice to have a little more ammunition for the old bolt-action. I feel safer now. I just wish you could come back with me."

He was quiet for a few seconds, then took my hands in his. "How about some dinner? Italian maybe?"

"Sounds delicious." I saw sadness briefly cross his eyes. Maybe I was talking too much about home.

"They have some great little restaurants down by Fisherman's Wharf," he said. "Let's head there."

Jimmy started to run and pulled me along with him as we jumped aboard a cable car. He paid our five-cent fares, and we found a couple of spaces open on the redwood planks that provided seating for tourists and San Francisco natives alike. Watching the city whisk by us, I almost felt like there was no war, no papas gone, no worries to go back to.

The conductor announced our stop, and as the cable car slowed, we jumped down onto the cobblestone street near the wharf.

Walking hand in hand, we passed little green and yellow boats returning home with their daily haul. The lone pop-bang of their single-piston engines had me almost mesmerized by the time we reached our destination.

Jimmy led me to a small door facing the bay. A sign reading "Frank's Italian Fare" wobbled overhead in the salty evening breeze. Jimmy placed his hand on the small of my back and led me up three narrow stairs to the little family eating establishment.

Frank greeted Jimmy by name and seated us by a curved window overlooking the glistening waters of San Francisco Bay. The red-checked tablecloth fell just about an inch above my knee, and Jimmy slid into the chair to my right.

"Order whatever you like, Lou," he said, squeezing my hand and passing me a listing of the night's specials. "Dinner's on me."

"Oh Jimmy, please let me treat you," I begged him. "You have helped me so much today. I couldn't have done it without you." Grinning, I held up the envelope from Morales Manufacturing. "And I have money for it now!"

"Let this be my treat," Jimmy said, caressing my arm. The bruises remained intact, but the red splotches had begun to fade like the afternoon sunlight. "Let's call it our first date."

My cheeks blushed as my butterflies joined in with their happy dance again. I returned the envelope to its safe resting place in my dress pocket. Smiling into his beautiful, caring face, I nodded and placed his hand in mine.

"I'd be honored, Ensign Jimmy, sir," I said. "Thank you."

We began our date with an appetizer of steamed shrimp cocktail followed by warm bread so fresh, it melted in our mouths. Jimmy ordered spaghetti, and I did the same, with extra meat sauce. We laughed as we tried to see who could slurp in the long strands of pasta the fastest. Jimmy won the contest, but I got the better end of the bargain as he gently wiped the red tomato sauce from my lips and replaced it with a gentle kiss.

As Frank took away our dishes, he brought us each a generous slice of homemade Charlotte russe. Jimmy placed a small bite on his fork and held it out for me to taste.

My lips curved around the silverware, and the flavor of buttery cake mingling with whipped cream and tart maraschino cherries danced across my taste buds. The dessert was the most decadent thing I'd ever tasted.

No, that was a lie. The kiss Jimmy gave me next was the most decadent thing I'd ever tasted.

"Let's take a walk," he said, pulling back from me which seemed to take all of his might. He handed Frank several bills, thanked him for a wonderful meal, and took my hand. He led me out of the restaurant, and we wandered through the shadows looming over the streets around us.

"See that building there?" Jimmy asked. "There's a golf course on the top of it. It's actually a government facility, but they put a golf course on the roof to fool anyone from finding out the true identity of the building."

"I saw that golf course from the air! They actually had people playing on it."

"They play in shifts. Kind of clever, isn't it?"

I nodded my head in agreement as we ran for a cable car headed toward the hill near the Presidio. Jimmy again paid our fares, and we settled into a couple of available woven, straw-covered seats in this particular cable car. The Golden Gate Bridge towered in its "International Orange" glory overhead in the distance. The heavy fog shrouded the streetlights and all but enveloped the bridge.

"Have you ever walked across it?" he asked.

Glancing at the formidable structure, I answered. "Never, but I'd love to tonight with you."

We jumped off the cable car at the top of the hill and walked across a grassy knoll toward the edge of the bridge. The wind whipped up the slope and sent a chill through to my soul. Jimmy gave the bridge attendant twenty-five cents for each of us, and we began the trek across the towering landmark. He was quiet for most of the crossing, and I began to think I had said something wrong. He seemed to be a million miles away. I stopped midway across, pointed out ships in the fog, and listened for the foghorns to blow. Below us, a little run-about jumped several waves and then whipped by what looked like two submarines.

"It must be the navy running maneuvers, or maybe submarines races," I joked, trying to lighten his mood.

Jimmy put his arm around me and said, "Lou, I need to tell you something."

I shivered in the chilly ocean breeze. He wrapped me in his arms for a moment to warm me, and it felt like something almost better than Heaven. It felt like home.

I turned my back on the churning waters below and faced him. He looked so sad.

Taking my hands in his, he stared at them for what seemed like an eternity. Finally, he glanced up into my questioning eyes.

"I told you earlier I'm on leave. That's true, but what I didn't tell you is that I'm what they call a 'Ninety-Day Wonder.' I never told you this, but I actually volunteered to join the navy. I knew I would be drafted, because of the census problem and all, so I figured since I was going to be called up anyway, I'd join the navy. I was sent to a college where they quickly train navy officers. They squeeze four years of training into ninety days, and then we get our Commission. That's how I got to be an ensign so fast and so young. My next assignment starts when I ship out. Tomorrow. To the south Pacific. The USS Enterprise."

My mind tried to comprehend and calculate what all those words meant. My shiver turned into a full-fledged shake that I couldn't control.

"The Enterprise?" I squeaked out. "I read about that ship in the paper. The Battle of Midway? The Solomon Islands? Guadalcanal?" My legs started to give way beneath my body. He reached out to steady me.

I can't lose Jimmy now. I just can't. I've only just found him again.

"That's right, Pipsqueak," he said, forcing a grin, trying to lighten the mood. But nothing could raise my heart back from the depths to which it had just fallen.

I was going to lose Jimmy again.

CHAPTER 28

During our silent walk back from the bridge, we found The Hydrangea Bed and Breakfast Inn run by Bess, a sweet, elderly lady from back east with beautiful wavy white hair. She only had one bedroom available, seeing as we were so late in finding a place, but she let Jimmy sleep on the divan in the gathering room.

I awoke, tossing and turning in the soft, fluffy bed, and stared at the morning sunbeams playing peek-a-boo with pink roses on the wallpaper across the room. I barely got any shut-eye, and Jimmy's news still tore at my heart. I closed my eyes and still saw the pain in his as he told me about his deployment. I hated to see him hurting like that.

Bess served us the finest breakfast west of the Mississippi River. Thick pieces of crispy bacon, buttery toast and fresh blueberry jam made from berries grown on the bush I saw outside behind her dainty, floral-print dining room curtains. We washed down our feast with two generous glasses of orange juice and thanked Bess for her hospitality and for taking us in so late.

Jimmy put his hand in his pocket to grab payment for my room and his divan.

"No, thank you, dear," she said, patting his hand and giving Jimmy a knowing gaze. No doubt, she heard our conversation before parting last night. "Thank you for keeping us all safe, young man. Please do the same for yourself."

We thanked her again and stepped out into the street shrouded with the last remnants of morning mist.

"We have a couple of hours before the rest of this fog lifts so we can cross the bay," Jimmy said. "Let's go by The Emporium. I want to pick something up."

"Okay," was all I could get out, sadness burrowing even deeper into my heart.

We walked by several stores not yet open for the day. I saw a yellow gingham pinafore in a dress shop and knew I needed to get the food and supplies back to Claret Lake—back to the kids.

A photographer on the street called out to us. "Two for a dollar. Two photographs. One for each of you."

"What do you say, Pipsqueak?"

His term of endearment was just the thing to lighten my mood.

"Yes, let's," I said with the beginnings of a genuine smile. "But I want a picture with both of us—together."

"Done," he grinned, pulling me close as we sat arm in arm and posed for the photographer. He worked his magic and several minutes later handed us two pictures and told Jimmy thank you with the same wistfulness as Bess had earlier.

Milk trucks, ice trucks, and navy trucks rumbled down the street beside us, quickly disappearing—just like the time we had left together.

"Promise to write when you can," I said, squeezing his hand. "And I'll do the same."

"No worries there," he replied. "I'll think about you all the time."

"Just make sure you think about surviving more." I tried to joke but came up short. "I'm going to miss you so much, Jimmy. I already do."

"It'll be okay, Lou. I'll be back before you know it." We stopped in front of Woolworth's Five and Dime, and he pulled me into a hug. The left-over Christmas decorations in the window tried to add a festive spirit to the bleak days ahead. But I couldn't dwell on that just yet. *I must put on a good face for Jimmy*, I thought. *He's the one going off to war.*

Tiny bells tinkled overhead as we walked into the store. Jimmy bought me an RC Cola and a nickel chocolate ice cream cone. He ordered himself a black cow and shared a spoonful of the smooth vanilla ice cream and tangy root beer mixture with me.

"Might as well do it up right," he said.

After our feast on everything sweet, we walked across Market Street toward The Emporium. Several elderly men sat on benches in a park near the store and flew colorful kites: dragon kites, box kites, and several homemade varieties. We watched them dart about in the sky and wished for some of their freedom to dance in the wind.

"Stay here and watch the show," he said. "I'll be right back."

I leaned against the cool brick of the storefront and got lost watching the tossing and turning of the kite show overhead. I pretended I was as flexible as their tails and could weather anything the wind might toss my way. Closing my eyes, I practiced remembering how Jimmy looked in his uniform. I didn't think I could ever forget it.

"Ahem," he said, stepping in front of me, blocking my eyes from the sun overhead. "I have something for you." He handed me a small yellow box wrapped with a pink and green striped ribbon. "In honor of your plane," he chuckled.

"Very funny," I said, rolling my eyes. I looked down at the small box resting in my hands, then back up at Jimmy.

"Open it."

I gently pulled on the ribbon until the box sprung free. My fingers traced the words on the box, "The

Emporium – San Francisco." Looking up at him, I saw him nod.

"Go ahead."

I took the lid off the box and peeled back a layer of thin white tissue paper. Then another layer. And another. Beneath it laid the most beautiful locket I had ever seen—a crimson heart outlined with a thin band of gold.

"I had them put our picture inside," he said, opening the locket for me to view. "When you see it, think of me and you, of our time here, and of all the good times to come."

"I promise I will wear it forever, Jimmy." He slipped the delicate gold chain around my neck, fastened the lock, and then turned me around to admire it.

My arms wrapped around him in a hug I didn't ever want to end.

"I know it's not a diamond, but I figure you have plenty of those," he whispered in my ear.

Looking up from the locket, our eyes met, and the world faded away into the distance. It felt like nothing existed beyond the two of us.

"This locket is more precious to me than any diamond could ever be," I said. "I love you, Jimmy."

"Well, that's the last of it," Jimmy said. "I hope you'll be able to take off under all this weight." The supplies filled the plane to the brim. In order for everything to fit, a new draftee removed the two rear seats and used a piece of metal to cover a hole in the floor left from removing the plane's bomb mount. Captain Hill had ordered his men to remove all armament before I was allowed to depart.

An ensign filled the plane with fuel, and I paid him out of my stash from Mr. Morales. I had a few gallons left over from the flight the day before and hoped that topping it off would last me and my pregnant airplane all the way back to Claret Lake.

Standing on Dock Seventeen, Jimmy and I embraced one more time, most likely the last time until the end of the war. I promised myself I wouldn't cry. I didn't want tears to be the last thing Jimmy saw from me.

"It's time to go," he said. "Before I ship out, I have to check in with Captain Hill and report on the crazy blonde-haired lady-pilot flying a Japanese airplane."

"You sure know how to make me laugh," I chuckled. I slid my hand into my pocket and came up with a present for him. "Now hold out your hand."

Jimmy obeyed, and I placed a beautiful, flawless diamond in his hand.

"For luck," I said.

He looked at me with questioning eyes. "But I thought you sold them all."

"All but this one. I kept it special for you. Moon tears are *very* lucky, you know, so it will keep you *extra* safe."

I thought I saw a shimmer of moisture in his eyes, but it must have been the glare from the sun.

"Thank you, Lou," he said, pulling me into one last hug. "I feel safe already."

"Ensign Hastings, time to go," Captain Hill yelled from the hilltop.

"Guess that's it. Take care, Lou. This has been the most fun I've ever had in twenty-four hours, except for your battle." He ran his hand over my arm. "You sure heal quickly. No one would ever know you faced a monster yesterday. I hate you had to experience that."

"I'm strong, Jimmy. I have to be. And I'll be strong flying out of here today." I hugged him once more and whispered in his ear. "Please come back. I'll be waiting for you."

"You bet I will, Pipsqueak," he said. "Fly safe."

And then he kissed me for the last time.

CHAPTER 29

The yellow and blood-orange hued sunset sprawled across the western sky like a mural painted by a French impressionist. I glanced at it and wondered if Jimmy was seeing it, too. Below me, I saw the tall slender lighthouse I noted on my flight to San Francisco. *Time to turn inland.*

I relished the feeling of flying free as a bird, swooping around mountains, banking left, dipping right, and being closer to Heaven than any of the mountain peaks below me. The wind whipped under one wing, then the other. After I adjusted the ailerons, the plane stabilized, and it was smooth sailing for the rest of the flight back to Claret Lake.

Bearing east, I spotted Mount Callisto welcoming me and my pink, green and yellow plane back to the tree-filled valley. Within fifteen minutes, I passed over its peak, glancing below to see newly emerged diamonds winking at me, congratulating me on my success.

In the distance, dirt clouds, courtesy of minimal snowfall this winter, trailed Clay, Murph, and Silver as they ran toward the dock to meet me.

Boy, are they going to be surprised at everything I have in this plane!

I gauged the wind, turned base and began my descent to the lake. The gusts flowing through the valley were from the south, but with the differential temperatures over and around the lake, a choppy approach was inevitable. Landing on pontoons proved easier than I thought, but with a fully loaded plane, my landing was far from pretty. The wings waggled like I was waving to the town, but truthfully, I was trying my darndest not to crash into the cold depths of the lake.

Flaps down, throttle off, angle of approach three degrees, cut power, and...we're down. No one except God heard my thoughts, and with His help, I landed safely without hitting any of the mallard ducks that decided not to migrate this winter. Pockets of snow blanketed a few shady areas of town, and stubborn patches of ice outlined the lake, but overall, it had been a pretty mild winter.

Puttering my way to the dock, I unlocked the canopy and tossed the rope by my seat to Clay.

"Tie her up good," I said. "And Murph, grab Mama's wheelbarrow from the shed. This plane's as full as a tick."

Murph craned his neck to peer into the back windows of the plane as Clay tied it securely to the dock. Silver ran in circles on the weathered wood, jumping and barking.

"*Holy mackerel! You aren't kidding, Lou!*" Murph shrieked.

A smile blossomed inside me as I heard his voice starting to crackle and change for the first time.

"How did you do it? Do you have any food in there? I am completely starved. We had to eat wood bark yesterday."

"Your savior has arrived, sir," I said as I jumped out and stretched my legs from the long flight. "Would you like filet mignon or caviar first?"

"Very funny," Clay interrupted. "But seriously, we have several kids at Doc's sick from not eating."

"Then let's unload this puppy and get to work." My stories of Jimmy would have to wait until later.

Eddie built us a large, billowing bonfire in the center of town, and everyone gathered around to receive their gifts. Clay and Murph helped me construct a spit and cooking platform out of leftover wood from the shed. We put a slab of beef that Jimmy and I got from a butcher near Fisherman's Wharf on the spit, and the smaller kids took turns turning it.

195

"Be sure to stay back from the flames, kids. Don't want anyone getting burned." The excitement of having real food in their bellies for the first time in days had them singing and dancing around in delight. It felt good, really good, to be able to provide for them.

In the distance, Rex leaned against the wall of the General Store. I ran to see him, leaping into his arms as he spun me around in the darkness.

"You were right! The moon tears saved us!"

"No, Little One," he said. "You did."

I hugged him and invited him to share in our bounty, but he simply nodded, placed me back on the ground, and backed away.

"Wait," I said, digging into my pocket for his present.

He took the leather knife pouch in his hand, looked down into my eyes, and placed one strong hand on my shoulder.

"Thank you, Little One. I will treasure it always." He slipped quietly away, disappearing into the night. I watched him go, wishing he would stay and hear my tales from San Francisco, but I knew he would be watching out for me from a distance. My guardian angel on Earth.

I turned back toward town to take in the scene, and my heart did a double flip, seeing the joy and happiness that a full belly brought to a bunch of parentless kids and a couple of old fogies. Even Doc and Aunt Mary danced their own form of the jitterbug in new, stiff leather boots.

"All is good in our little corner of the world again," I whispered to Silver who had not left my side all evening. Petting the soft fur on his head, I looked with grateful eyes toward the west. Thoughts of the conflict that raged beyond the California coast filled my mind, and the cold of the evening began to sink in.

"Thanks for your help, Jimmy. I pray you are safe and warm tonight."

CHAPTER 30

Spring of 1945 arrived before any of us could believe it. Soon the pears, walnuts and animals would reappear, repeating the cycle of the seasons. It had been over a year since Jimmy and I spent our time together in 'Frisco. He had written me six times, each letter a little direr than the one before. He wrote of days brimming with hard work and nights filled with fear of the next attack. He received the letters I sent him and said they brightened his days. I felt that I did so little compared to the important work he was involved in, but I knew I couldn't dwell on that or depression would surely set in.

The view from atop the watchtower did its best to take my breath away. The sun had just finished its morning stretches, and contentedly put its shine meter on full bright for the day. Placing my hand over my brow, I squinted to see if I could see the town.

Claret Lake emerged from the shadows and looked so innocent, so untouched by the war. But ever since returning from 'Frisco, my tower time couldn't help but be filled with thoughts of Jimmy.

After getting the planeload of supplies, the town had run like clockwork. Everyone performed their chores like they were second nature. The General Store was stocked, and the girls were getting to be pretty decent cooks over at the restaurant. The younger girls were handling the laundry like the professional laundries in 'Frisco, and the boys were even having some luck hunting, since they had warm clothes and some vegetables to go along with the meat they caught. We even took time one afternoon to slough off some stress and play in the lake.

"Hey, Lou, I'm here," Eddie called, interrupting my thoughts. He climbed up the final steps of the ladder to relieve me until nightfall.

My gaze fell to his smiling face. "You look happy today, Eddie. What gives?"

"Just excited to be on watch and not in the water. Never been one for being in the wet stuff. Don't know how you used to swim every day."

I gathered my pack and headed for the ladder. "Well, if you change your mind, come on up to the lake."

"Thanks, but no thanks. I'll just hang out here in the Fort." Eddie liked to pretend he was Robinson Crusoe.

"Well, have fun. See 'ya tonight," I said, shimmying down the ladder toward Silver who had chosen to stay below and play in the leaves.

"Let's go, boy," I said, giving him a bear hug. "Time to have us some fun!"

"Clay, hook up that ski rope in the pump house to the underbelly of Pinkie." Clay and Murph nicknamed the emissaries' plane "Pinkie" upon our arrival back to Claret Lake. "Let's make some use of the gas that's left and go skiing."

"Aye-aye Capt'n Lou," he said, sending me a salute that would have made Jimmy proud.

"Who's first?" I asked, hands on my hips, standing on the dock next to Pinkie. All the boys raised their hands, and all the girls clapped for them.

"Remember that when you're behind a boat, there's a wake you have to compensate for. But when you're behind a plane, there's no wake, so no compensation is necessary. When you're up on the skis, it's completely smooth in front of you."

"Anything we should know before you take off?" Murph asked.

"Definitely," I said. "Hold on tight, and be sure to watch out for the prop blast until I pick up some altitude. I learned to ski behind those float planes that Papa's friends used to fly up in. Takeoff speed was about forty knots, or forty-six miles an hour, so I was up skiing before they actually took off. In this plane, it will be faster. That means you really have to be holding on good. Once you're up, you'll have to bend down so your knees are at a right angle, like you're sitting in a chair, and lean back, or the speed will flip you over. I'll fly Pinkie around the lake once for each skier. Then I'll land, and you can switch off."

Clay bravely stepped up to take to the water as a guinea pig. Becky gave me a thumbs up when he was ready to go. She seemed to have gone through a growth spurt after getting some good food into her system.

I crawled into Pinkie's pilot seat, mentally went over my checklist, and buckled up before opening the canopy another inch or two.

"*Clear*," I yelled, then started the engine. I ran it up for a couple of minutes and checked the flaps and carb heat. There was no need to worry with the transponder, but I kept the radio on.

Pinkie inched forward, and then lurched into full takeoff mode. She didn't flinch even once when the ski rope became taut and Clay rose up from the water.

"He's up," Barbara radioed.

"Roger that," I replied, lifting the nose of the plane and keeping its altitude just about thirty feet above the water. I banked to the left to begin a circle of the lake and saw Clay waving up at me. Straightening out over the center of the lake, I gave Pinkie a little more juice and made it up to about fifty knots, just fast enough that Pinkie wouldn't stall. That made for some good skiing.

"He's still up," Barbara reported.

"Roger," I replied. Turning back toward the dock, I began my descent and saw Clay grinning from ear to ear. Touchdown was smooth since for once, Mother Nature cooperated and decided not to bother us with any wind.

Puttering toward the others on the dock, I opened the canopy and laughed at the kids clamoring to ski after they saw how much fun it was.

"Who's next?!"

CHAPTER 31

April, 1945

The first half of the day continued to be reserved for schooling. Aunt Mary was not nearly as strict as before, and we were taking more of a role in our studies. We tried to make sure to do our lessons and to learn at least three new things each day before the brass dismissal bell rang at noon.

For the first time since Jimmy left, we had a patient-free doctor's office, so Doc spent his days trying to coax fish out of the lake. Clay, Murph and I sat on the dock, dangling our feet in the water beside Pinkie before I headed to the watchtower for another shift.

"Do you think you'll ever fly her again?" Murph asked between licks on a grape lollipop, one of the treats I brought back from my trip to 'Frisco.

"I don't know," I said. "There's not much fuel left, maybe twenty or thirty gallons tops. No way I could make it back to 'Frisco on that."

We sat in companionable silence, no one wanting to talk about what we would do if or when we ran out of supplies a second time.

The kids voted to hold a school prom in late spring, so Clay, Murph and I opened up Mama and Papa's dance hall and wiped away the spider webs and crawling creatures that had claimed it as home for the last three years. Fern and Barbara made chain daisies out of scraps of paper and the last of the glue we had in the supply closet at the schoolhouse. Becky ran in with a handful of paper clips, erasers, acorns, and various seeds and laid them gently on the floor in front of me.

"Are these decorations?" she asked, looking at me with hope in her little brown-flecked eyes.

I carefully examined the smorgasbord of knick-knacks she had so painstakingly collected.

"These are the *best* decorations I've ever seen, Miss Becky." I shook her hand and elicited a smile that would light up the night. She squealed and ran to tell Eddie of her success. Clay and Murph chuckled at her delight.

"It's just a bunch of pins, paper clips, weeds and junky shards of paper," Murph said.

"It may look like a pile of junk to you, but to me, it looks like a priceless centerpiece." I transformed the desk we placed underneath an old stained glass window into a food and drink table, complete with Becky's collection.

Orange poppies and purple wildflowers that I found during a quick walk by the lake added the perfect touch to complete her centerpiece.

I turned back to survey the dance hall. It looked like a genuine prom paradise. Mama's fancy glasses and plates filled the teacher's desk that we borrowed from the schoolhouse. A big sign overhead, painted with paint left over from Pinkie's makeover, read 'Welcome to Prom.'

Bev and Julie brought in a bean casserole and a big vanilla sheet cake with a thick layer of chocolate frosting. Tommy arrived with a tray of pears and grapes, and Murph delivered a bowl of walnuts to round out the fare.

"It looks beautiful, everyone," I said. "Now go get your best party duds on and meet back here right after sundown."

Excited feet scampered out the door and down the stairs, running toward home, excited about having a party.

"I'll see you guys later," I said to Clay and Murph. "Gotta head up to the tower."

"But you can't go tonight," Murph said. "It's Prom night. You *have* to be here."

"I wish I could, but I really need to make sure I take my shift. What would everyone think if something happened tonight?"

"They would think that you should've gone to Prom," Clay said. "Come on, Lou. One night won't make a difference."

The battle that had been brewing inside my head all day began to intensify. I knew I had my duty, but didn't I deserve to have a little bit of fun like everyone else? In all these years, I had never spotted more than a few American military planes and that blasted jet. Maybe one night would be fine.

"Okay, guys, I'll go."

"Woo-hoo, Lou!" Murph pumped his fist in the air. "That's swell!"

"But I have to go up and let Eddie know so he won't wait for me later on and miss the party himself."

Eddie was excited that everyone including me would be at the prom. He and I jogged back down the hill into town and parted ways at my house.

"Sure wish Jimmy was here to go with me," I said to Silver who greeted me by the door, wagging his tail. We walked into the kitchen, and I grabbed a cracker to tide me over.

Oh, heavens. What on earth am I going to wear? I guess I'll have to put on a dress. I looked through my small closet, but it was devoid of anything appropriate for a prom, so I tried Mama's closet. I must have grown a few

206

inches since she left for Richmond because I couldn't wear anything she had anymore either.

Rummaging through the old cedar trunk by the foot of Mama's bed, I tossed aside my baby blanket and a crocheted tablecloth before I found a dress I didn't remember ever seeing before. The pale yellow linen frock looked to be knee length. It had a jeweled bodice and was lined with white homemade lace around the neck and cap sleeves. My fingers ran across the soft, silky fabric of a sky blue sash lying delicately atop the garment. Lifting the dress and sash from the trunk, I saw a pair of inch-tall white lace-up dressy shoes and an envelope addressed to Mama lying underneath them. The return address was Abilene, Texas.

I turned the envelope over, pulled out a letter yellowed with age, and read the words of my grandma:

Dear Dolores,

I am sending you the dress and shoes that you wore for your first school dance. They was in my trunk by accident, I guess. I always thought you took it with you to Californee. Anyway, I hope Lou'll be able to wear it one day.

Be sure to put it in a cedar trunk so bugs don't get ahold and eat it.

Love you dear,
Ma

"Well, I'll be darned," I said, sinking into the feather bed with the dress on my lap. Looking heavenward, I clutched the dress to my chest and whispered, "Thanks Grandma. I'll take good care of it. I promise."

CHAPTER 32

Thunder rumbled in the distance as dusk nestled into the valley. I grabbed an umbrella before leaving the house and walked toward a night of fun and frolic. Silver pranced beside me, proudly wearing his special blue and gold bandana I had brought him from 'Frisco. Glancing back toward the path to the tower, I felt a twinge of guilt but reminded myself that everything would be okay.

"We can play hooky for one night, can't we boy?" Silver gave a quick "*woof*," and we raced toward the party.

Turning toward town, I saw the dance hall shining from the glow of a few dozen candles Aunt Mary had lit and placed in the windowsills around the room. Walking up the stairs, I paused to look down at the dress that even I admitted looked really pretty. I straightened a few persistent rogue wrinkles as a shrill whistle invaded the moment.

"You sure clean up good, Lou," Murph said, walking up the stairs behind me and whistling again. I gave him a playful swat on the arm as he gave me a once-over. Believe it or not, he extended his arm to escort me into the prom.

The door opened ahead of us, and Clay stared straight at me. "You look...beautiful," he said as he stepped down to take my other arm.

"Why thank you, Clay," Murph said in his best imitation of a girl. "How nice of you to notice."

Clay swung a fist at Murph and growled, "I wasn't talking to you, idiot. I was talking to Lou."

"Oh, sure you were," Murph chimed in once more, and then feigned pain as he received another punch in the arm from Clay.

"Okay boys, take it easy. It'll muss my dress if I have to break up a fight."

A streak of lightning lit up the darkening sky as we entered the door to another world, just for this one night.

The fairyland that greeted us was filled with decorations, food, and the rest of the kids. The sweet smell of cake, confections and fruit wafted through the dance hall. My old trumpet and Clay's guitar waited for us by the teacher's desk, so we settled in and started to play a few songs all the kids knew. Everyone found a partner and swung them around the open dance floor. Feet glided light as feathers around the dance hall, soaring along with the spirits in the room. We sang some old songs, two or three new ones, and we made up a few along the way.

After about an hour, we took a break from playing and had some of Aunt Mary's pear punch to soothe our parched throats. Out of the corner of my eye, I saw Doc standing by the door. He poured a tiny stream of amber liquid from a small etched silver flask into his glass of pear punch and downed it all in one swig. He stumbled out the door and into the shadows of the moonless night.

Bev and Julie grabbed Clay's guitar and my trumpet and started to play. It was a basic tune, but we had been teaching them how to play during some of the free time we'd had since things got better. They had been practicing all week long, especially Bev. Clay held his hand out to me, and I placed mine in his. He twirled me around a few times, and then settled into a slow dance as Bev and Julie switched to a slower tune.

"You've done good, Lou," he said. "We're all proud of you."

"Thanks, Clay," I said. "But I couldn't have done it without you and Murph. You two are my rocks. When Jimmy had to leave, you really stepped in, and I can't tell you how much I appreciate it."

We danced and twirled around the room, and I thought I saw sparks, but it must have been the lightning flashing outside the window panes. I never felt that way about Clay, and certainly not for Murph. In fact, it appeared Bev was sweet on Clay. She had been watching us the entire dance with a look of longing in her eyes as she strummed the chords of a love song on Clay's guitar, singing like a mournful angel. I took the lead and led us over toward her.

"I'll take over on the guitar," I said to Bev. "You two go cut a rug."

Clay blushed a little, and Bev jumped at the chance to be in his arms. After one time around the dance floor, they finally mustered the courage to look up at each other, and I was sure I saw sparks fly between them.

Just as they started to inch closer to each other, Doc burst through the door, screaming and hollering up a blue streak. I was afraid he might indulge in a little too much celebratory whiskey, but there was no way he was going to ruin our prom. I laid down the guitar, rose from my chair, and motioned for Clay. We marched toward Doc as the aroma of whiskey grew stronger in the air.

"Doc, come with us. You've had too much to drink. Why don't we go get some coffee at the restaurant and sober you up some."

"But I seen 'em! They're out there, gettin' ready to attack us!"

"Who's out there, Doc?" Murph said, walking up and taking Doc's other arm to help escort him out.

Everyone followed us out the door, and as soon as our feet hit the dirt street, the bottom fell out of the sky. Rain drenched the town. A white flash of lightning zigzagged across the darkness as Doc turned and pointed up to the sky.

"It's the enemy! They're here!"

CHAPTER 33

My stomach twisted and turned as I stared into the moonless night. Lightning struck in the distance again, lighting up the dark expanse of sky for a brief moment, and we all saw the drifting objects floating above town.

"It's just some weather balloons, Doc," Aunt Mary said. "Even I can see that."

"Maybe so, Aunt Mary," I said, patting her on the back of her now drenched red lace shawl. "But I need to check my spotter's guide, just to make sure. I'll be right back."

Stupid! Stupid! Stupid! I thought as I ran toward the tower. *How could I have been so incredibly stupid!*

Hitting the side of my temple with one hand as punishment, I ran as fast as the muddy path allowed. Silver sprinted through the storm by my side, although I had let him down as well. I knew I shouldn't have gone to the prom. Of all nights for something to happen, it would be the night I shirked my duty.

An uneasy feeling of nausea invaded my belly, and the twisting and turning soon turned to churning. I hoped those balloons weren't what I thought they were, but the packages dangling about fifty feet or so below them weren't normal.

Running up the hill to the tower, I glanced down and realized Grandma's dress was totally and completely ruined, not to mention the mud covering the formerly white lace-up shoes. I looked up at the sky again, asking penance for more than the ruined dress and shoes.

Sorry, Grandma. It's my fault. It's all my fault.

Reaching the tower, I started to climb the ninety-four rungs of the ladder. I had counted them so many times in the past years that each rung was committed to memory. Silver stood guard below, the hair around his neck standing on end. Each lightning bolt seemed to get closer, and I started to climb faster. Only four more rungs to go. The air crackled just before a streak of lightning flashed directly in front of the tower, and the accompanying thunder momentarily deafened me. Instinctually I covered my ears with my hands, and my feet slipped from the wet ladder.

I screamed as I started to fall, then instinct kicked in for a second time. Ignoring the ringing wreaking havoc in my ears, I grabbed the closest rung with two clenched fists and stopped my fall as I heard my two pinky bones crack. I abruptly stopped, and my body swung from the ladder.

Concentrate, Lou. Think. Breathe. Pull it together.

My feet scrambled to find the ladder, and after regaining what little footing I had, I began to climb again. Finally pulling myself into the tower, I collapsed, curled up in a ball on the floor, and gave myself exactly five seconds to cry like a baby and to feel sorry for myself.

This is all my fault.

Sitting up, I grabbed the spotters guide and the emergency flashlight. Running my fingers across the images on the pages, I saw that the balloons were not any of the enemy aircraft that were listed. I searched for the flyer that came in the mail earlier in the week. Rummaging through the papers in the desk, I found what I was looking for. Standing near the edge of the tower, looking out into the dark stormy sky, I tried to locate the balloons to get a closer look.

Just north of town, lightning struck one balloon, and it exploded into a blazing ball of fire.

Oh, Jesus. This is not good.

Running my fingers over the drawings on the flyer, I stopped over the last one and looked below the balloon drawing to the box of explosives dangling below. The balloon outside matched the flyer perfectly:

"JAPANESE FIRE BALLOONS"
BEWARE – EXTREMELY DANGEROUS

Fire balloons thirty feet in diameter are filled with hydrogen. They carry multiple incendiary devices on lines sixty feet below that double as fuses. The enemy launches them from their own territory, and they fly in high winds at approximately thirty thousand feet. Seventy-two hours after the balloons are launched, the fuse ignites, destroying the balloon and lighting the lifting hydrogen on fire. These new weapons have been sighted on American soil since 1944.

*WHEN SPOTTING THESE BALLOONS,
USE EXTREME CAUTION.
REPORT ANY SIGHTINGS IMMEDIATELY.*

My trembling hands flung papers into the air as I tried to locate the radio. I finally found it in the bottom drawer and pressed the talk button.

"*Army Flash! Army Flash! This is Claret Lake Tower! We are being bombed by fire balloons! Over!*"

Silence

"*Do you read? Over.*"

Silence.

"*Army Flash! Is anyone out there? Over!*"

Silence.

I screamed out in frustration and threw the broken radio on the floor. *No one is going to come help us, and possibly worse, no one knows we're in trouble. Even the tribe is too far north of the flames to be able to help.*

The flaming shards of balloons exploding over the tree line drifted down just north of town, away from the lake and toward the trees ripe as kindling for catching fire.

Why do these blasted winds have to be from the north? They're going to blow the bombs right over Claret Lake!

I scurried down the ladder as fast as my heeled feet could go, ignoring the pain in my fingers and gripping the flyer between my teeth. As soon as my feet hit the ground, an explosion rocked the valley. Silver whimpered and leaned firmly against my right leg. Instinct brought my head up to the direction of the blast, and I saw a fireball rising to the sky, a line of trees on fire beneath it. *The bomb must have detonated when it hit the ground.*

Every curse word I'd ever heard rattled through my brain. Glowing ash fell from the sky, singeing Grandma's dress and scalding my skin. I ran toward town, Silver close behind. I heard my name on the wind as I saw Clay and Murph running full speed toward us. The heavens dried up the moment Silver and I reached them.

"We've got trouble," Clay said. I could see Murph shaking in his boots. "Looks like we've got us a fire, and the winds shifted a couple of minutes ago. Now the fire's headed toward town. We sent the girls, Doc and Aunt Mary to your place to get in the rowboat and take it as far out in the middle of the lake as they can. The wind whipped up good over the last few minutes and with that fire headed toward town, we were afraid they'd get caught in it if they tried to head south on foot. At least in the lake, they stand a chance at survival."

"What are we going to do?" I screamed. "This is *all* my fault. I never should have gone to the prom. I should have been on watch."

"Well, that doesn't do us any good now, does it?" Murph said.

"Watch it, Murph," Clay interrupted, wiping my sooty face with his shirttail. "Okay, Lou, pull yourself together. What do we do? There's not a single drop of rain left in this storm, and it looks like it didn't even touch the area north of the lake."

I tried to gather my wits as I untied Grandma's blue sash, ripped it with my teeth, and handed it to Clay. "Wrap these fingers for me, okay?"

He bound my throbbing pinkies to two adjacent fingers with the shreds of blue, rain-soaked silk, giving me a few seconds to formulate a plan.

"What do we do, Lou?" Clay asked again.

I took a deep breath.

"This is war. So we *fight*."

CHAPTER 34

The diamonds glowed a deep red across the lake, reflecting the essence of the flames. The scent of scorched wood permeated the town. Clay, Murph, Silver and I ran to the dock to meet up with the other boys. Clay broke off to retrieve the two-way radios from Papa's shed and passed them out to everyone. Thank goodness they all worked and the batteries seemed good.

"The flames are getting closer," Clay said, glancing over my shoulder toward the north. "How are we going to fight this?"

"Those things up there are Japanese fire balloons." I wiped my brow of the sweat that hadn't stopped since Doc screamed about the enemy being here. "So far, I think I've seen about ten explosions over Claret Lake. Eddie, take one of the emergency radios and go back to the tower. Look out for any more balloons and let us know as soon as one appears. Do your best to determine its speed, location, altitude, and bearing."

"Roger that," he said, turning to run to the tower.

"Ralph and Tommy, you two try to get to the water tank on the hill. If you skirt the lake, you should just be able to get far enough west to circle around to it. Connect the emergency hose and drench the area around the tank. Hopefully it will keep the fire from going any further west."

"What about us?" Clay looked scared now, his eyes as big as saucers. Murph appeared to be in shock. I coughed, choking on the pungent, soot-filled air.

"You two go toward the airfield and start digging a trench as fast as you can. Take the shovels from the shed. Hopefully it will serve as a big enough firebreak to keep the fire from spreading east."

"I'll use the tarpaulin from the boat to form a storage tank inside Pinkie," I continued. "I'll fill her up with water here at the pump, fly over the worst parts of the fire and dump the water on it from above. Hopefully we have enough fuel left in her for a few runs of this. Now let's get going."

I felt a tug on my pant leg and turned around.

"What about me, Miss Lou?"

"Becky! What in tarnation are you doing here? You're supposed to be with Bev and the others out on the lake!" I tried to see through the darkness to the center of the lake, murky from the ash-laden sky. There was just enough light from the fire in the distance to make out the silhouette of a rowboat filled with people in the middle of the water.

"I didn't want to leave without you," she said, hands on her hips, determined to be of use. "I wanna be like you. I wanna help. I wanna be strong, just like you."

Clay and Murph shook their heads, ran toward Papa's shed to grab a couple of shovels, then disappeared into the darkness only lit by the light of the leaping flames in the distance.

Taking a deep breath, I gathered my wits again.

"Okay, Becky. I could use some help with the pump house here. I need the water strained and drained so that when I get back from a run, I'll have water ready to load back into Pinkie, and Ralph and Tommy will have enough for the water tank on the hill."

"Roger, Miss Lou," she said, saluting and turning to run toward the pump house.

"I can't worry about her. I just can't," I said under my breath, repeating the mantra and opening Pinkie's canopy. *How am I going to get water onto the fire from this plane?* I thought. Looking in the vacant area behind the pilot seat, I caught sight of the metal piece covering the area where the bomb attachment was removed in 'Frisco.

Bingo!

"Becky, hand me that tarpaulin and those two pieces of rope on the dock." It was a good thing Doc and Aunt Mary left them behind when they took the boat.

Pulling the four corners together, I cinched the tarpaulin with one piece of rope, formed a tight slip-knot, and pushed the rope a few inches through the hole in the belly of the plane.

"Now jump onto the pontoon and hand me the long end of the rope," I said. Grabbing the braided rope, I wound it around the pilot seat. I cut a small hole in the part of the tarpaulin that faced up, shoved in a hollow piece of metal broken off of an old oar, and used the other piece of rope to secure it.

Perfect—a makeshift water tank.

Becky returned with a hose connected directly to the pump's strainer. She handed it up to me and I filled the tank to the top. I handed the hose back to her and hoped not too much water would slosh out the pipe during flight.

"Now Becky, you stay here, okay? Here's a radio so we can keep in touch. I don't want to be worrying about you. If the flames get too close, swim for the island. Silver will stay here with you. He is super-strong, so if you get tired, just hold on to him. If the wind shifts and blows the fire toward the island, then grab some tule reeds from the far side overlooking Mount Callisto, get into the water, hang onto them, and swim. Silver will help you, won't you, boy?" I scratched him behind his ears.

223

"Yes ma'am, I'll do just that, Miss Lou," she said, patting Silver on the head and not looking the least bit frightened.

CHAPTER 35

"*Watch out for those fireballs!*" I screamed into the radio.
Flames leapt in every direction as the relentless winds
gained strength. "I'm going around once more then it's
back to get more water. Have the pump ready, Becky," I
radioed as I banked Pinkie away from the fire that
engulfed the entire valley north of town.

Eddie checked in. "Okay, it looks like the fire's
spreading to the south-southwest at about five miles an
hour now."

"Roger," we replied in unison.

"With the winds blowing like they are, we're
looking at a heap of trouble if we don't head it off before
McGregor's Hill."

The cockpit was an oven. The heat from the inferno
felt like it would boil the sweat off my brow. "I'll drop
whatever water I can carry in this flying bucket on the
parts of the fire approaching town."

After making the drop, I roared toward the lake at a
hundred and twenty knots. I leaned the engine,
executing a perfect teardrop approach to the lake. Gusts

buffeted the plane as it descended into the valley nestled between the mountains.

"Three, two, one," I muttered as the pontoons met the lake once more. "Taxiing to the pump station," I radioed.

As I pulled alongside the dock, Becky jumped onto the pontoon and retied the slip knot around the sides of the tarpaulin poking out the hole in the plane's belly. Leaping back onto the dock, she tossed me the other end to secure. She had grown up so much during the past few years. A distant memory of her tiny body clinging to me when her mama and papa left with the others invaded my mind.

Sliding the canopy full back, I breathed in ash-laden air that brought me back to the task at hand.

"It's funny how you know how to fly a plane but still don't know how to drive a car," Becky said, handing me the hose and running back to turn on the pump.

I wiped the soot and beads of sweat from my face with an old cleaning rag I found on the floorboard and filled the tarpaulin with another round of lake water.

Becky returned from her task and crawled up the wing. "Aren't you scared up there, being near the fire and all?" Her brows furrowed in grooves much too deep for a ten-year-old.

"I don't think I've ever really been afraid of anything, Pumpkin, except losing this town," I said, ruffling her matted brown locks.

The radio began to crackle, and then it blared. "Lou, we need you to be our eyes! Over."

I did a quick check of the water pumping into the plane and saw the pump house continued to pull through for us. It proved to be a smidge ornery this morning, but after a few kicks and curses, it started working again.

I got on the radio and touched base with the boys manning the water tank on the hill just west of the airport.

"Tommy? Ralph? How are things at the water tank? Over."

"We're hanging in there," Ralph said. "It's really hot up here. Tommy has one hose aiming water to the north, and I'm taking the south and southwest. The flames to the east are getting bigger, but you have a better view of that from above than we do."

"I'll get back up there as soon as I can and let you know how it looks. Give me a few minutes."

I turned back to Becky who heard the whole conversation and headed back to the dock.

"Gotta go fight that fire now, honey. Please go turn off the pump for me so I can head out." I checked to be sure the rope remained secure and climbed back into the cockpit. A quick tap on the gas gauges told me this would be the last trip Pinkie could make, so I had better make it worth it.

Becky gave me a quick salute, and I started my last taxi of the war.

CHAPTER 36

"Okay boys, this one has to count. I'm running out of fuel. Only got one run left in Pinkie. Over."

Gaining altitude off the lake, my reflexes kicked into gear. I could practically fly Pinkie blindfolded now. No questions. No second thoughts.

"Things seem to be fine at the water tank," Tommy radioed. "The tank is completely empty, but the ground is soaked and no flames are anywhere near us."

"That's good news," I said, relaxing for a second before Clay radioed in.

"Lou, we need you over here near the airport. The flames are getting away from us."

"On my way," I said, flying as fast as I could toward the tiny airport. I saw the flames dancing higher than before. The boys had done a good job clearing the place of leaves and digging firebreaks, but this one area was the biggest fire pit left.

"It's almost sunrise," I radioed. "I can see some clouds moving in from the west from up here. Maybe we'll get lucky and see some rain."

"Maybe so, but right now we need some old fashioned fire-fighting action," Murph interjected.

"I'm going to go north and turn back like I would to land at the airport, then I'll douse the biggest part of the fire with all the water I've got."

"Roger that," Clay said.

Dawn began to flirt with the darkness as I flew north of the tiny airport by the mountains. No large planes ever landed here, only tiny, little planes. Just before the war, they started accommodating planes that were a smidge bigger, like a twin-engine Beech or a Beech Bonanza. They shaved almost a hundred and fifty feet off the top of the hill at the north end of the runway so pilots could approach and land. If you kicked up dust when you came in, then your position was spot-on.

Just as I prayed I wasn't coming in too low, the sun decided to make its entrance for the day. I could just make out the shaved-off hill in front of me and breathed a sigh of relief. I lowered Pinkie's nose, and dust surrounded the plane, the wind whipping through the divot in the hillside, tossing up rocks that pinged off the metal pontoons underneath me. To my left sat the old Quonset hut I hadn't seen from this altitude since before the war began. The dirt strip was a perfect firebreak, so I headed for the area just west of it.

"Approaching the monster," I radioed. "Three, two, one—here we go." I pulled the rope that would untie the slip knot, releasing the fire-fighting lake water and waited for the "Woo-hoo" from Clay and Murph.

Silence.

"It didn't work," Murph cried. "Nothing happened."

I pulled on the rope again. Nothing.

Glancing out the port window, I saw the culprit. The rope had snagged on the rivet that had cut me all those years ago.

"Okay, boys. The rope is caught on a rivet and won't budge. Gotta go around once more and figure out how to uncatch it."

"Hurry, Lou," Murph's voice crackled over the radio. "It's coming right for us."

Think, Lou, think.

Glancing around the cabin, I searched for something I could use to dislodge the rope. Nothing.

If I can bank the plane back and forth a few times, maybe I can get it to loosen up.

I wrapped the rope around my wrist several times to secure it and began my maneuvers. Banking left was no problem. Banking sharply right, I heard the engine chug.

"Come on, Pinkie, don't fail me now," I shouted. She sputtered and clanked but did not cooperate. My asthma took Pinkie's lack of cooperation as a go-ahead to hijack my lungs. I tried to breathe, but the air felt like it had been sucked out of the plane.

Pinkie started to dive toward the ground, bringing me closer and closer to an early death. Glancing out the front window, I wheezed, sputtered, and saw the propeller had completely stopped.

This is not good.

I had heard it said you have flashbacks of your life right before you die. Mine got in line. Instinctively I grabbed the locket Jimmy gave me and stroked it with my fingers. Things I hadn't thought of in years flooded my mind: petting Seabiscuit up in Covolone when I only came up to his knobby knees, Jimmy hitting a golf ball through an airplane's fabric wing and us trying to fix it before we were found out, sling-shotting woodpeckers to sell their topknots for five cents apiece to the Indians for their headdresses, my first airplane ride in the yellow tandem two-seater, Jimmy taking care of me after the rattlesnake bite, when Amelia Earhart was lost and my heart broke for the first time, when Jimmy left and my heart broke for the last time...

"Lou, what the heck are you doing? Pull up! Pull up!" Clay screamed over the radio, jolting me back from my near-death flashbacks.

My mind latched onto the flashback of Jimmy rubbing my ankle after the snakebite. He tamed my asthma then, so I rubbed my ankle and imagined Jimmy's hands taming it again.

"Thanks, Jimmy," I said, finally managing to take a full, deep breath. I glanced quickly toward the west.

Think, Lou, think. The gas must have drained out of the wing that was up during the last banking. I banked the plane the other way and tried to restart the engine. We both sputtered and choked, then Pinkie sputtered again. She wheezed once more, and then her engine finally caught. I gained a little altitude but had to do so with the right wing at an odd angle.

"I have to keep this wing up, so I'll be flying in circles until I can get into position. Good news, though. With all the twisting and turning, the rope isn't caught on the rivet anymore." I unwound the other end of the rope from my wrist and slid the canopy back another few inches.

"Okay boys, let's try this again." I approached the shaved off hill once more, aimed for the center of the fire, leveled out the plane and started my countdown.

"In five, four, three, two, one." I jerked the rope and felt the slip knot give way. The water fell, drenching the worst part of the fire with a planeload of water.

"Gotta head back to the lake. Pinkie's out of fuel," I radioed as the engine quit for the second time. I prayed the bucket of bolts would coast all the way back to the lake.

"We're all drenched, but so is the fire! You did it, Lou!" Clay hollered, laughter in his voice. I heard Murph cheering in the background.

"Glad to hear it boys," I said, wiping the sweat from my brow. "See you back in town."

CHAPTER 37

September, 1945

I can...breathe. I smiled between smooth, rhythmic strokes in the robust Pacific waters west of the Golden Gate. My spirits soared high, like my destination—the bright orange structure looming ahead. Each rise and fall of the salty, foamy ocean waves penetrated me to the core. Each sea breeze filled my soul with the strength and energy of life and the sea. Each kick kept me moving forward, toward the weathered rocks jutting out from the champagne shore. Toward Jimmy.

"Keep going, Lou," he said, standing on the rocks, smiling in the morning light, and holding out a bar of fresh Ghirardelli chocolate as my reward. "You're almost here."

"Be there in a minute," I yelled as a rogue wave covered my head. I reemerged from the whitecaps and treaded water, laughing as miniature streams trickled down into my ears. I shook my head, diving deep into the next wave like a harbor seal. Underneath me, a giant brown and white speckled sea turtle glided by, flitting and swerving like a submarine doing maneuvers.

Swimming again after all those years gave my body an ache—a good kind of ache—an ache of achievement, an ache of happiness. I planned to swim one mile along the San Francisco shoreline every single morning. Three hundred and sixty-five days a year. Not doctor's orders, but *my* decision.

Swimming allowed my thoughts to wander, gave me time to think: to think of Mama, Papa and Sheriff Gabe returning to Claret Lake after the victory in Europe, just in time to hear my speech at graduation; to remember the bittersweet return after the war for those who had been drafted and their families; to mourn those who didn't make it back.

Washington sent Mama a letter after V-E Day admitting they made a mistake recording the census numbers for Lagune County. The letter read, "We are gravely sorry for any inconvenience this incongruence might have caused." Little did they know what a life-changing experience that one zero had spawned.

I sliced through the waters heading toward shore and thought about my move to San Francisco during the summer. When they announced the war was over, people from every walk of life celebrated non-stop in the streets, on the rooftops, on boats and frigates in the bay, and in tickertape parades throughout the city. Victory permeated San Francisco with a level of happiness, joy and celebration that can't be imagined or recreated, except when I recall the elation and satisfaction that came from saving Claret Lake from the brink of starvation and the ravages of a fiery invasion.

I thought back on the war years a lot and what I had learned about myself. Those years taught me that I was strong—a survivor. Mama and Papa saw my inner strength from early on. I finally knew it's who I truly was.

I loved living and working in the big city of San Francisco. Gumps hired me on to work in their jewelry department until college started in the fall. They manufactured fine jewelry on the third floor, and I delivered it city-wide: jade, rubies, treasures from the Far East, and diamonds, of course.

My mind drifted to college and beyond. I thought about following in Amelia's footsteps and training for my pilot license, considering all the opportunities and adventures that would allow.

When I moved to 'Frisco, I took to the streets every day, hoping to see Jimmy step out of a crowd of people. He sent a letter that made it through about three months ago saying he would be out of touch for a while on some secret missions in the Pacific, but not to worry. I worried until last week, when he stepped out of a sea of white uniforms on North Point Street and into my life again.

"Hurry up, Lou. Get over here."

"Be right there, Lieutenant Jimmy, sir." I licked the salty water from my lips and broke my stroke to send him a watery salute. Things happened fast during the war, and he returned home with two silver bars riding atop each shoulder that winked in the morning sun. My thoughts were only of him as he held up a small box in the palm of his hand.

Time to start the countdown. Five, four, three, two, one...

I made shore and dug my feet into the warm grains of sand. Every time I ran up the beach toward Jimmy, my heart soared to new heights. Each day I loved him more than the day before. He was my rock, my stronghold, my soul.

I shivered when the sea breeze met my moist skin. Jimmy wrapped me in a towel he had warmed on a large rock in the sunlight and gave me a bear hug. The warmth of his embrace was more than a thousand sunbaked towels. The musky scent of brine, salt and seaweed surrounded us, and the gulls laughed as they dipped and swerved in their dance overhead.

Before I was ready, Jimmy broke the hug and sat me down on a brown rock by my feet. He reached deep within his coat pocket and withdrew the box with which he had beckoned me back to shore.

"I have a present for you, Pipsqueak." He handed me the small package wrapped in blue and yellow paisley paper, held in place with a white silk ribbon.

"For me? Why Jimmy, how sweet of you!"

His eyes focused on the package, then he raised them to meet mine.

"Go ahead. Open it."

My fingers gently pulled on the silk and the soft ribbon fell to my lap. I shook, not from being cold, but from the anticipation of what awaited me inside the package. I gently removed the wrapping paper and handed it to Jimmy. The lid lifted off easily, and I folded back several thin sheets of paper to find a second box covered with cream-colored velvet.

"What's this?" I asked, brushing the soft flocking with my fingers and lifting the smaller box into my hand. I glanced up to see Jimmy smiling.

"Open it."

The box opened with a click. I looked down, and my breath caught in my throat—not from asthma, but from awe. I reverently held the box and its contents in my shaking hands and looked up into his eyes.

"It's stunning, Jimmy. Absolutely breathtaking."

He took the necklace, looped it around my neck and clasped it. "When I was away during the war, after I saw you in 'Frisco, I held that diamond you gave me every day. Carried it wherever I went. Never let it out of my sight. It was my talisman, my good luck charm, my link to you. I swore I would never be without it."

My fingers stroked the smooth edges of the diamond, hanging in its new home around my neck.

Taking his hand in mine, I smiled and said, "You never will, Jimmy. You never will."

AUTHOR'S NOTE

I didn't know when I sat down to dinner a couple of years ago with my cousin, the real Lou, that I would leave that table a different person. Listening to her stories, I was enthralled with this woman with whom I had just connected a few years prior. She had experienced so much—grasped life by the horns—and never took guff from anyone. I realized she was the person I aspire to be. Throughout that visit and others that followed, she regaled my husband and me with stories of her youth and growing up during World War II in a remote town in northern California. It was a different time—a different world—filled with people that did what had to be done in order to survive.

Moon Tears is based on many of the real-life experiences she shared with us during our visits. Numerous occurrences in the book actually happened to her: the asthma, the daily swims across the lake, the emissaries' visit, the mistake in the census, the kids having to run the town when everyone left, the rattlesnake bite, the surgery with no anesthesia, becoming a member of the tribe, learning to ski behind an airplane, becoming a pilot before she could drive, and the existence of the diamonds that came from the slopes of the mountain near her hometown. Through her stories, I also learned about many aspects of World War II that I never knew existed: the Volunteer Aircraft Observers (of whom Lou was one), the existence of the German Bund, the circuit riders, the Old Man's Draft, Victory mail, the building in San Francisco disguised as a golf course, the use of diamonds in manufacturing during the war, Treasure Island's role during the war, the Ninety-Day wonders, and the Japanese fire balloons that landed on the west coast.

In researching the vocabulary used in the 1940's, I enjoyed discovering and incorporating terms from that era, but my favorite was "giggle water," another name for alcohol. During one of our visits with Lou, she introduced us to a wonderful neighbor of hers, Leo, who fought in World War II. He shared with us letters he had kept that were written by his buddies. It was a joy to read these gems from the past and see the use of terms like "swell" and "jeepers"—just the way I'd always imagined young people of that era would write and speak. Additionally, I learned that the phonetic alphabet for aircraft tail numbers were different in the 1940's than they are today.

It is my hope that this book will inspire people to delve a little deeper into their own families' histories, to uncover the stories their relatives hold dear, and to pass them on to future generations.

To learn more, please visit:

Cavanaugh Flight Museum:
www.cavanaughflightmuseum.com/
Dedicated to educating the public on aviation studies and preserving America's aviation heritage.

CollectAir Gallery:
www.collectair.com/
Dedicated to educating the public about the differences between war planes, and home to the "A Friend or Foe?" museum.

1943 Aircraft Warning Service Film: *Eyes Aloft*
www.archive.org/details/TF1-3315
Honoring the work of the Ground Observer Corps of the Aircraft Warning Service.

Victory mail educational website:
www.postalmuseum.si.edu/victorymail/

Military Factory:
www.militaryfactory.com/aircraft/detail.asp?aircraft_id= 443

For information on the Aichi E13A Jake, the plane upon which Pinkie was based.

Turner Classic Movies: *Water Bugs*
www.tcm.com/search/?text=water+bugs&type=allDb
1941 MGM short film featuring skiing behind an airplane.

~ ~ ~

Moon Tears is a work of historical fiction. It was inspired by a series of real-life events and is set in the fictional town of Claret Lake, California. The main character—Lou—is based loosely on the author's cousin, and the other characters are fictional.

ACKNOWLEDGEMENTS

I am deeply grateful to so many people for their help and support in getting this story told. First and foremost, I am grateful to Lou—for sharing your life stories, allowing me to write about them, and inspiring me to grasp life for all it's worth. I also am indebted to my wonderful critique group—Bill Burton, Laney Nielson and Murray Richter—who caught things I never would have seen and brought Jimmy to life in more ways than one! And many thanks go to my dear friend Angela Cavener, my favorite author, whose enthusiasm and talent inspired me to take up this amazing adventure of writing. Special thanks go to Nathan Reinhardt for a fabulous cover design; to Michelle Snowden, Cindy Rodella Purdy and Mari Barrett for valuable input explaining what it feels like to have an asthma attack; and to Mellisa Dempsey for helping me solve a pivotal issue I wrestled with for months. I appreciate all the work and many laughs my copyeditor provided—thanks Kevin. And a quick shout-out goes to Tina, Mike and Emily at Delish Bakery in Charleston, South Carolina who saved a table for me to work at when I was in town and kept the key lime muffins coming.

A special thanks goes out to SCBWI for providing a network of professionals eager to help me write the best story I can—many thanks to Carol Barreyre, Cindy and John Purdy, Patricia Vermillion, Nancy Keene, Cynthia Wildridge, Kay Honeyman, Linda Bishkin, and Tanya Cretella.

Thanks also to my cousins—Loraine, Diane, Raquel, and Tony—for sharing your mom and grandma when I was in town so I could write this story based on her childhood. And to Leo and Ellie for sharing your letters and hospitality with us. Thanks go out to Cathy, Bambi, Sarah Catherine, and Mae Mae for reading my stories and being so excited about them, to Ruth Holder for the fabulous spa days and life discussions, to Lisen Kintzele and Diane Kelly for your encouragement and friendship, and to Polly Holyoke for your kind words.

Many thanks to the Native Americans with whom I consulted (who wish to remain anonymous) for teaching me about tribal language and culture so that I could portray them both accurately and authentically, to Steve Remington of the CollectAir museum and gallery for his help understanding how spotters pinpointed different military aircraft, and to Alexander Peake at the Cavanaugh Flight Museum for teaching me about the Aichi E13A and the differences between war birds.

To my sister, Happy, brother-in-law Mike, amazing nephews Lex, Elliott and Ben—a special thanks for being so supportive, for being my cheering squad, and most of all for letting me be such a big part of your lives. To my mom and dad—thanks for sending me to wonderful schools and making me do my summer reading, even though I fought it all the way up to the last minute!

Most important, I am grateful to my husband Eric—my champion—who believes in me and everything I do and gives me the freedom to follow my dreams. Thank you for putting your pilot hat on and teaching me how to take off, land, and read all those instruments. Thanks for your never-ending support throughout the writing process, fixing many a dinner when I couldn't break away from the computer, and reading, re-reading and re-re-reading my numerous revisions. And most of all, thanks for the adventure of a lifetime.

Moon Tears came to life because of you all—thank you from the bottom of my heart.

ABOUT THE AUTHOR

M. M. Frische has been fascinated with World War II stories since childhood. She would sit and listen for hours on end to her great-uncle's tales of parachuting into Normandy the night before D-Day. Many years later, she met her cousin—the real Lou—and discovered an entirely new set of stories about the war. *Moon Tears* is her first novel. Having been a reluctant reader in her youth, she was excited to discover (many years later) that she had only been covering up her true love of reading and now finds it hard to put down a book. She is also a professional photographer and loves to travel, having been to all fifty states and around the world. She lives in Texas with her husband. Please visit her website at www.tenstorybooks.com.

43969366R00156

Made in the USA
Charleston, SC
13 July 2015